FIRE
DREAMS

The firefly was blindingly bright in the daylight, coloured vividly with gold and orange and scarlet. The midday sun dazzled over its shiny scales and it was difficult to make out any more detail for it had already started its strange dance, that bizarre flickering at high speed between positions. The Pyromancer gave an order and the door to the cage was opened. The firefly switched between a high-tailed prancing and a predatory crouch and dashed out into the crowd.

Screams now. Like one enormous living creature, the crowd retreated. The beggar lifted his hand to shade his eyes. The firefly was diverted towards the dais. It had seen the prisoner.

POINT
FANTASY

FIREFLY
DREAMS

Jenny Jones

■SCHOLASTIC

Scholastic Children's Books
Commonwealth House,
1–19 New Oxford Street, London WC1A 1NU
a division of Scholastic Ltd
London ~ New York ~ Toronto ~ Sydney ~ Auckland

First published by Scholastic Ltd, 1995

Copyright © Jenny Jones, 1995

ISBN 0 590 13375 6

Typeset by TW Typesetting, Midsomer Norton, Avon

Printed by Cox & Wyman Ltd, Reading, Berks.

For Nesta, with love

CONTENTS

PRELUDE

"Well, what about Wincy then? We could stay with her, she'd be in charge—"

"No!" Jarred Brooke slammed his fist down on the table. "For the last time, the *very* last time, you are not going to Bricus! Not this summer. Your mother and I have to be away and there's the shop—"

"Sam and Molly can look after the shop," said Laura. "They don't need us."

"You have your studies. I'm not having you junketing off round Bricus for the summer at this stage in your education. And I don't see why your cousin Wincy should have to put up with visitors during a time when she's bound to be extremely busy."

1

Laura sighed. Wincy was lady-in-waiting to Countess Philomena of Bricus, and during the festival would no doubt be in attendance at all the balls and galas and ceremonies.

"Randall would be around," said Darius stubbornly. Randall was Wincy's brother. "He could show us the sights."

"For Heaven's sake, Darius! I'm not having you pestering Randall either –"

Jarred stopped suddenly. He looked across the table towards his wife. "Cytheria, what is it?"

Darius and Laura turned to their mother.

Cytheria Alderwood sat at the kitchen table and clutched it with her hands so hard that the finger-nails showed white.

"What's the matter?" Jarred moved round the table and laid his hand on his wife's shoulder. "Cytheria, what is it?"

She shook her head suddenly. "I don't know. A goose on my grave, something, nothing…" Her words trailed away. Then she sighed and picked up her napkin once more. "I'm sorry. I wish Wincy would write. It's so long since we heard from her. She's so like her mother, hopeless at keeping in touch…" There was still something very stressed about her voice and Laura, for one, felt a cold shiver of fear.

Cytheria was still speaking. "All these changes at Bricus, the new Pyromancer… I wish I knew what it meant, what was happening to everyone there."

"It's such a long way away. Although I must say it's strange that there have been no travellers since the new Pyromancer was sworn in. But I understand Lord Lerris is excellently qualified for the role," said Jarred.

"So we've been told. But what does anyone actually know of the man? Turning up like that out of the blue, when old Lord Renfrew was so ill. You'd think he'd known Renfrew was dying."

"Renfrew was *eighty*! Everyone knew he was on the way out."

"If you let us go to Bricus, we could bring you news," offered Darius.

"Darius, go to your room. Right now. Not another word." When Jarred's eyes snapped like that, no one, not even Darius, argued.

Darius pushed his chair back from the table and stood up. The door banged behind him.

Laura followed. She always went everywhere with him. She was his twin, after all.

That night, Laura couldn't sleep. She was infected by her mother's anxiety. An unreasoning dread, the shiver at the back of the mind, beyond the reach of logical thought, kept her on edge.

Something had happened. That night, while they sat round the dinner table, something terrible had happened. Cytheria had been most affected, but Laura had sensed some of it too. It was to do with Wincy, with what was happening in Bricus.

If only she could ask her mother! For years Laura had tried to get her mother to talk about her strange intuitions, but Cytheria had always refused. "It's not appropriate in a shopkeeper's wife," she would say, severely. "Don't nag, Laura."

Such questions invariably irritated Cytheria. Who else could Laura ask? Although Wincy and Randall were their cousins, they were much older than the twins, nearer to their parents' generation. But Laura had always felt close to Wincy, during her rare visits from Bricus. She and Randall had been in the habit of sending both twins birthday presents and Laura had delighted in the series of ornamental glass bottles that arrived every year.

That night she slipped out of bed and crossed the room to the shelves where the bottles stood.

She never drew the curtains at night and it was a full moon. In the cold light, she picked up one of the bottles and held it up at the window.

Through the curved and cut glass she looked at the face of the moon, that familiar collection of irregular shadows and planes.

It had changed. This was not the moon she knew.

It looked like Wincy. The broad forehead, the soft dark eyes and the curving mouth. And Wincy looked frightened, something Laura had never seen before. The dark eyes were wide, the mouth no longer laughing.

Something dreadful, something terrible was happening. Suddenly breathless, Laura put the bottle back. She picked up another one and, with hands that were rather shaky, held it up to the moon.

A different face this time, one she didn't recognize. An old man, and he too looked as if he were desperate. Another bottle, another face: a young boy, his lips drawn back in a grimace.

Each of the bottles seemed to hold a different person. Old, young, male and female, they had nothing in common but this appearance of terror.

She went back to her bed and pulled the covers up high. If only she could talk to her mother about it! What had happened, what had gone wrong?

What was going on in Bricus?

CHAPTER 1

Capture

Marrin took the kitten from Philomena and threw it out of the window. He was out of control and Philomena had never seen him like this before. She was more frightened than she had ever been in her life.

She wasn't going to let him see it. Philomena backed slowly towards her dressing-room, where Wincy waited, and at the doorway she drew a small green phial from her pocket and gave it to Wincy.

If Marrin was going to be violent, she could not afford to stay.

She watched Wincy smash the phial on the stone floor and a great cloud of poisonous smoke billowed out. She heard Marrin coughing and choking and under cover of the confusion she slipped away down the spiral stairs to the back garden door, leaving Wincy behind.

At the bottom of the stairs Philomena stopped. Wincy had not followed her. Perhaps she'd been caught. Philomena hesitated. All their futures were at stake here. All their friends and families and colleagues. They would be lost for ever. This row with Marrin was the least of it. She could not even afford to try to help her dearest friend.

Philomena took another phial from her capacious pockets and unstoppered it. She laid it carefully on the ground outside the door, where some pansies were growing. She kept hold of the stopper.

Some time later the little kitten, who, in the way of most cats, had survived the fall from the second-floor window, came mewing round by the back door, asking to be let in. Getting no immediate response, it investigated the clump of pansies and was intrigued to find a tightly stoppered glass phial tucked away in the undergrowth. There were only a few drops of liquid in it, enough to sparkle in the harsh sunlight.

For a while it patted the glass bottle to and fro with its paw and then someone came and opened the door for it and it forgot the pretty shiny thing under the pansy leaves.

But later still that night, after all the fuss had died down and something like calm had descended over the Earl's palace, someone else came searching through the undergrowth.

A very old man, dressed in a velvet frock coat with tartan trousers, creakingly bent down and picked up the phial, putting it into his pocket with some satisfaction. He spent a while poking round amongst the leaves and stems but at length gave it up.

His face, as he left the palace grounds through a secret gate in the wall that no one else knew, was frowning.

He'd expected to find two bottles there, but there had only been one. Wincy hadn't made it.

She'd been caught by the Pyromancer, Lerris.

The execution was due to take place only a few days later. All of Bricus turned out to see it, the aristocracy and the townspeople, the urchins and the beggars.

One of the beggars hung back from the rest of the crowd. He waited in a doorway to one side of the square. Far away the procession from the palace had come to a stop. The trumpets blared once and a half-hearted cheer went up from the crowd.

The ceremony began. The speeches and the denunciations took some time. Great scrolls were read to the crowd by officials in golden uniforms. There had been a certain emphasis on the legal process in the city recently: justice had to be seen to be done.

The prisoner was brought forward to the front of the dais. Her hands were fastened together behind her. A soldier shouted something and pushed her so that she fell forward on to her knees.

It looked painful, that action of falling to the knees. The beggar flinched in sympathy. His mouth shaped silent words, a curse of some kind. He knew why Wincy was there, although he was too far away to hear the proclamations. She'd been caught. Their only hope was that the Pyromancer wouldn't attempt to use aquemancy. A feeble hope at best: Lerris was known to be investigating the water-witches' arts before the row with Philomena.

The crowd was silent, watching the proceedings. There was nothing the beggar could do. Beneath his ragged clothes, his filthy hand clutched a surprisingly sharp and bright knife. He might disable one of the guards, two, if he was lucky and no one got in the way. But there were scores of them, he had no hope of getting her out of it.

He edged forward. The crowd seemed very tense, hardly daring to move or breathe in case they were noticed. They stood aside from him as if he were no more than a shadow.

There was another fanfare. The Pyromancer, a tall figure dressed in flowing golden robes, stepped to the centre of the stage, just behind the prisoner. He raised his hands to the sun and an audible moan ran through the crowd.

The beggar halted. He knew what was going to happen. As he expected, the gate to the Earl's palace swung open. A strangely constructed cart rumbled out across the cobbles, pulled by horses. The crowd immediately drew back to let it pass. There was a cage on the cart, a cage made of thick bluish pipes. Glass, thought the beggar. Glass filled with water, so that the firefly won't escape.

The firefly. It looked much as he expected, but it was still a shock. He breathed a sigh, and a woman standing nearby glanced sharply at him.

The firefly was blindingly bright in the daylight, coloured vividly with gold and orange and scarlet. The midday sun dazzled over its shiny scales and it was difficult to make out any more detail for it had already started its strange dance, that bizarre flickering at high speed between positions. The Pyromancer gave an order and the door to the cage was opened. The firefly switched between a high-tailed prancing and a predatory crouch and dashed out into the crowd.

Screams now. Like one enormous living creature, the crowd retreated. The beggar lifted his hand to shade his eyes. The firefly was diverted towards the dais. It had seen the prisoner. For a while it was almost still, as if waiting for a signal from the Pyromancer.

Lerris raised his gauntleted hand and brought it sharply down.

The firefly began. It moved towards Wincy, crouching and prancing like some ancient courtly dancer. It liked to play. With a rush of smoke and flame it suddenly incinerated one of the hangings around the dais. The material flared briefly and then crumpled into a fall of smouldering ashes. Slowly the monster moved towards Wincy and at every breath the hangings turned to drifting ash...

The beggar was muttering something, almost unconsciously, beneath his breath. But he knew there was nothing he could do. He could only watch. This was up to Wincy. He had to trust that she could still practise her skills. He couldn't bear to contemplate what would happen if she didn't manage to escape.

It worked. He knew it, because when the firefly reached the woman he cared about, it stopped.

For Wincy was no longer there. The chains and manacles clattered to the ground. There was nothing there, no fall of ash, no smoking remains, but a puddle of water dripping over the edge of the dais.

The firefly breathed on the water, and some of it evaporated in a cloud and the beggar gave a

11

curious kind of half-moan. And then the firefly whirled round, screaming with fury.

The Pyromancer Lerris stood very still, his face unreadable behind the sunburst mask.

In front of the vast square, crowded with people, the firefly shimmered and shook and eventually retreated back into its cage.

The Pyromancer turned his back on the crowd, unhurriedly returning to the palace. His cloth-of-gold robe trailed over the stone behind him. The guards lined up in an orderly formation and followed the Pyromancer back into the glass-roofed palace.

There were no further fanfares, no display of power and pomp. The officials and the magicians and the guards left the dais and returned to their quarters. The crowd milled around, muttering dangerously, disturbed and puzzled by this strange failure. It took the beggar some time to fight his way through the throng to the dais.

He was too late. He missed the old man, who had caught the few drops of water on the edge of the dais in a small bottle. He had slipped the bottle into his pocket before disappearing swiftly into the crowd.

The beggar turned abruptly and was very soon lost in the crowd.

CHAPTER 2

Bricus

They managed to squeeze into Bricus before the gates closed for the night. Although they were both tired and hungry, it meant a lot. They'd been on the road for over two weeks. There had been a few lifts, but not many. Darius and Laura were exhausted.

They were also hot and thirsty. This was nothing new. They had been hot and thirsty for most of the journey. They'd never known a summer like this one. Everyone they met on the way agreed it was unusual. A heat wave, with no rain, no wind, nothing except a furnace of a sun, beating down on them all.

Inside the city wall Darius and Laura stood still

as the gates clanged shut behind them. A thousand faces, noise, dirt, colours. They smelled dung and fire and dinners and drains and sweat. The narrow streets were crammed with people.

For the last five miles Darius and Laura had been promising themselves a long, cool drink as soon as they reached Bricus. And although they'd run out of money long ago, they knew there would be drinking fountains in the streets. Randall had said so. "It's hot there, a real desert city, but the river runs pure and clear and there are gardens everywhere and drinking fountains on every corner. No one goes thirsty in Bricus."

Standing by the city gates Laura scanned the web of streets and alleys that radiated away from them. They saw nothing resembling a drinking fountain anywhere.

No gardens, either. Again that shiver. What had happened here? This was nothing like Randall's description. "Perhaps we don't recognize Brican fountains. Perhaps they look like something else…" Laura suggested. And it was true that the city was unfamiliar in every way. The dark skins of the crowds, their long, flowing robes in hot colours of rose and orange and gold, were all exotically strange to Darius and Laura, up from the country without their parents' permission.

"We'll make straight for Silver Street," said Darius, confidently. "They don't seem to go in for public amenities in this part of Bricus." He sniffed. "It all seems rather shabby. I suppose we should have brought more money."

Laura said nothing. She'd thought all along that they should have brought more money. But Darius had brushed aside her suggestions as usual. "Nonsense," he'd said. "If we're careful and use our wits, we'll have more than enough."

But they hadn't. The two purses of silver they'd brought with them had vanished away. Everything was more expensive than they'd expected, food and drink especially. "It's the drought," people said. "There's not enough for us, either."

Darius told Laura that it would be all right once they were at Bricus. Their cousins would take them in and then they'd be able to relax and enjoy the festival.

Laura let him think this was all his idea. Darius was happiest when he was bossing her around. But really, it had been she who had initiated their escape from Sam and Molly.

She didn't tell him why. She couldn't forget the fear in Wincy's face, and all those other faces, reflected in glass. She didn't understand what was happening, but she knew one thing.

Wincy needed them. They had to get to Bricus without delay. There was an emergency, something terrible had happened. It was bad luck and worse that their parents had forbidden it.

She looked longingly at the lemonade seller at the side of the road. His stall was hung with baskets full of fruit, and iced water founted through a glass container. Her throat was parched, her legs wobbly with tiredness. "Can't we ask him for some water?" Laura asked. "Surely –"

And they had both started to cross the road towards the man when two soldiers in scarlet uniforms, their faces concealed behind bronze visors, marched up to the man and started giving orders.

Laura saw the man begin to argue, and then one of the soldiers pushed the cart over, and all the water spilled out into the dust.

She groaned. She saw the man hustled away, and a number of children suddenly materialized from the crowds and swooped on the scattered lemons.

By the time Darius and Laura got there, they had all gone.

"Silver Street," said Darius decisively. "Let's stop wasting time. We need to find Randall and Wincy."

This was what Laura wanted to do more than anything, but she could see no street signs anywhere. She frowned. There was something badly wrong here. There were no decorations in the streets, no bunting or posters announcing entertainments, nothing to show that this was the Brican Summer Festival.

"Well," she said, anxiously. "Which way do we go?"

Darius glanced down at her. He was a lot taller than she was, although they were twins. He hadn't understood her anxiety to get to Bricus. Sure, he wanted to go to the festival himself, but Laura was being really strange about it, as if there was some desperate reason for being here. But she wouldn't tell him, whatever it was. For the first time ever, she had a secret she wasn't sharing with him.

Still, she did look tired. "Come on," he said bracingly. "It can't be far. Near the west gate, Randall said. We'll soon find it."

He pushed his way through the edge of a crowd round some public stocks and Laura trailed behind him. All the while Darius kept up a flood of chatter. She knew what he was up to. He was trying to divert her from the sight of those three men, ragged, bloody, emaciated, chained there.

"Well, we made it, didn't we? It'll be soft beds tonight, water and lemonade and Brican wine and Cousin Wincy's salmon soup. There'll be kittens to play with..."

Laura was hardly listening to him. She'd heard it all before. He always went on like this. As if she was a baby or something. He thought she'd be upset by the men in stocks, too. And it was true that she thought it cruel and vindictive. But she was a country girl, she'd seen animals killed, she knew that life was hard.

If you did wrong, you were punished. It was fair enough. They were probably thieves or slavers or something.

They turned away from the stocks, trying to bear towards the west. Their way was held up by the mass of people. They kept their eyes open for fountains of course, but that was useless. And the street signs were impossible to decipher. Some had been defaced, others were in a dialect Laura and Darius didn't understand. Most streets had no sign at all. It was going to take for ever. They hadn't realized how big Bricus was. Laura pulled away from Darius and planted herself in front of an old woman carrying baskets of washing.

"Excuse me," she said. "Do you know the way to Silver Street?" The woman's eyes were frightened. She looked past Laura as if she didn't exist and hurried on.

Laura stared after her, puzzled. She'd heard that the people of Bricus were friendly. Cousin Randall had always gone on about how people chatted, how lively it was, what fun...

Well, there were inns on every street corner. People spilled out of the doorways, sprawling on to the filthy cobblestones. Laura had to dodge to one side to avoid a drunken man staggering towards her. He looked as if he was about to be sick. If this was Randall's idea of liveliness, she didn't think much of it.

And still nothing to drink. Laura sighed. Perhaps she should ask someone else. But the next person she tried, another, younger, woman behaved much the same as the laundry woman. People didn't want to speak, they didn't want to help two strangers lost in the city.

This hot, stinking, crowded city with its frightened people, its bewildering maze of streets. No festival, no celebrations or fun that Laura could discover. Something was badly wrong here and she still didn't know what it was.

In the end Darius stopped a man who was wearing a coat of scarlet and yellow ribbons, woven tightly together.

"Over that way." The man spoke briefly, nodding to the right. His hair was greasy, hanging in heavy rats' tails. "You're miles off. Ask again."

It was depressing. More than that, it was worrying.

At the corner, Laura stopped. Something made her turn back and look at the man in the colourful coat. He was talking to another man in uniform, and as she watched he looked up and caught her eye.

There was no friendliness in his glance. She felt chilled, although the night was hot and sticky.

"Come on," said Darius sharply. "What are you waiting for?"

She shrugged and followed after him. But something about that man stayed with her, nagged at her attention. He was evil, she thought. That man in his silly coloured coat and greasy hair. He meant harm.

Trailing after Darius, she knew there was no point in telling him.

They had to ask again, several times. They tramped on, increasingly weary in the stifling heat of the city, through the winding streets, getting further and further away from the crowds, and all the time Laura's feeling of unease increased. She wondered if they were being followed. But no matter how quickly she turned round, she never saw anything suspicious.

At last, after many false turnings they found the narrow alleyway called Silver Street.

There was nothing in the least silvery about it. High walls, blank and windowless, rose above them. It was very dark. A foul stream of muck clogged a channel in the middle of the alley and piles of rubbish clung to the walls. There was only one street lamp at the far end, hardly enough light to see the house numbers.

In the end they found it. There was no bell or knocker at cousin Wincy's door. Darius thumped on it, first with his knuckles and then with the handle of his knife.

The sound echoed back at them. They knew at once, without doubt, that the house was empty.

And there was someone watching them. A dark shape emerged from the gloom to stand under the lamp at the far end of the alley, a tall man in a cloak. He was soon joined by several other figures.

Laura was frantic. "Oh, Wincy *must* be there, she has to be there…"

Darius thumped again, more determinedly. "Well, really! Where can they be at this time of night? There must be someone in, servants at the very least."

He glanced back at Laura and then his face changed.

"Run!" he shouted at her and pushed her shoulder.

He was so clumsy! She was off balance. She fell headlong over a heap of rags at the side of the alley, and at the same time heard the rush of heavy footsteps towards them. She tried to struggle to her feet, but her ankle was caught, held by something.

Cursing, she tried to release herself. And then someone flung a stinking piece of sacking over her head and she heard a voice hiss, "Be still!"

She knew that voice. She nodded briefly against the sacking and stopped moving, trying to work out what was happening to Darius.

She heard shouting, not Darius's voice, but other rough men's voices. And then scuffling, the

21

sickening sounds of fighting, flesh against flesh, grunts and curses. Heavy boots slid through the muck just in front of her nose.

And then there was silence. She started to say something.

"Shhhh," came the voice in her ear, soft as breathing. And then, only then, did she hear the heavy tread of feet as the men tramped off down the alley.

CHAPTER 3

Randall

The sacking was flung back. The alley was quiet, completely deserted. There was no sign of Darius or of the other men.

The pile of rags against the wall shifted and stood up. Laura found herself staring at her cousin Randall.

Or was it him? For a moment she was unsure. This filthy stranger bore no relation to the elegant, devastating young man who had drifted in and out of their lives ever since she could remember.

He was dressed like a beggar. The silvery blond hair was darkened with grease and dirt, the pale skin was shadowed by the beginnings of a beard. His clothes looked as if they'd been found in a gutter.

But the dark grey eyes frowning at her were entirely familiar.

"My God, Laura! What are you doing here?"

"Randall! Why are you dressed –?" And then, only then, she thought of her brother. "Where's Darius? Those men – what's happened to him?"

Randall pulled her to her feet. He looked grim, his eyes darting up and down the alley. "This way," he said, not answering her question. He hustled her a little way along the alley and through a door she had not noticed. It led to a passage which ran beside the house where he and Wincy had lived.

The passage opened out into a walled garden, overgrown with roses and clematis and ivy. The mass of greenery crowded in over them, blocking out the narrow glimpse of sky, so far away.

Randall took her through the garden, not into the house, but to the shed which stood at the end. Inside, there was a strong smell of geraniums and tomatoes. Trays of seedlings and flowerpots cluttered the floor. Randall bent down and dragged a sack of compost to one side.

A trapdoor. Still silently, without a word, he lifted the cover and motioned for Laura to go down the stairs.

She heard him close the door and then the sound of dragging again. He'd clearly got some way of manoeuvring the sack of compost back into position on top of the trapdoor.

It was pitch dark with the door closed and at first she could see nothing. But then Randall struck a match, and the small flame lit a low-ceilinged room, impossibly crammed with junk.

There was a lantern hanging on the wall, which he lit, a candle standing on a table. There were boxes and cartons and crates stacked against the walls. Some were open and she saw books, materials, saucepans and candlesticks. One wall was entirely hung with pictures, and many more canvases leaned against the side. With an increasing sense of dread, Laura recognized a portrait of Wincy there.

In the centre of the room there was a table and chair. Beyond that, a couch piled with cushions and rugs showed where Randall had been sleeping.

What had happened?

Laura suddenly realized how tired she was, how completely exhausted. She pulled out the chair and sat down. There was so much she didn't understand, so many questions to ask that she didn't really know where to begin.

Randall flung himself down on the couch.

"Now," he said. "Why have you come to Bricus?"

"But what about Darius?" she said. That was her overwhelming worry. "What's happened to him?"

"You first. He'll be all right. There's nothing we

25

can do about Darius for the moment. What are you doing here?"

She made an effort to hold her thoughts together. "We're here for the festival." She avoided his eyes. "We left a letter for Mum and Dad. They said we couldn't come, that it was too far to travel on our own, but that's ridiculous. We're fifteen, after all. Old enough to get married or go into the army, although they wouldn't let Darry do that either –"

"Go on." He looked bleak and for some reason that frightened Laura more than anything.

"It's partly your fault!" she flared and then wondered at her own daring. "You were the one who told us all about it, about what it was like here! Parties, you said. Dancing and street theatre and feasts and music. Of course Darry wanted to come! What did you expect?"

"Your parents will be frantic!"

"No, they won't. They've gone on a trading expedition to the Western Isles, they'll be gone for at least six weeks. They left us in charge. Honestly, Randall, it's just not fair! We're responsible enough to look after the shop for all that time, but too immature to come to Bricus... Does that seem reasonable to you?"

He stared at her. It was unnerving. "Think about it. Were they right to trust you with the shop?"

"Don't be so stuffy!"

He wouldn't let it go. "So who *is* looking after the shop?"

"Sam and Molly as usual. They said they could manage –"

"Really?"

It was always difficult to mislead Randall. Laura sighed. "All right, so we did run out. But we left a note –"

"Oh, God."

"Randall, what's wrong? Who were those men? Why are you dressed like that and where's Wincy gone?" Looking at his face, she thought, not for the first time, that perhaps they'd made a dreadful mistake, coming to Bricus. "Why are you living *here* and not in the house?"

"It's a long story." He stood up and went to a shelf opposite the door. "You'll be hungry, I suppose, you're always hungry, aren't you?" He took down a half loaf of bread, rather stale, and some cheese wrapped in greaseproof paper.

Laura suddenly realized that she was shaking. She pushed away the plate he put on the table in front of her. He must have noticed something because he suddenly leaned over her, and laid his arm across her shoulders.

"Hey, come on, Laura. This isn't like you."

"It's Darius!" she cried. "I don't know where he is, I don't know what's happened to him –"

"He's been pressed."

"What do you mean?" The continuing bleakness of his tone did nothing to comfort her.

"The palace is in need of soldiers. Any young men in non-essential work are required to do a turn in the militia. Strangers are seized straight away. Your dear twin will be trying on his new uniform as we speak."

"Darius isn't a soldier! He'll hate it!" But then she wondered if that were true. Darry was always nagging their father to send him to military college.

"It won't do him any harm." Randall moved away from her and she felt cold again, lonely and tired.

"But I don't understand! Why are you dressed like that? And where's Cousin Wincy?"

"You've arrived in the middle of a crisis, Laura. It couldn't be worse." He stood up and began to pace up and down the small room. "In brief, the Earl has had a brainstorm. Heaven knows what has possessed him, but the general consensus is that the new Pyromancer, Lord Lerris, has more than a little to do with it. Marrin has banned aquemancy. The edict was issued three weeks ago." He passed his hand over his forehead. "God, less than a month! Marrin has repudiated his wife, he's outlawed all water-witches, he's building up the militia with a view to ridding the city of everyone who ever tried to predict the rains!"

"Why?" This seemed like madness to Laura.

"Marrin is convinced that water-witches are traitors, all in league with his wife Philomena –"

"With his *wife*? He thinks his wife is a traitor?"

Randall nodded. "It all came to a head last Saturday. The militia were sent out to search the city, to arrest all water-witches. Wincy and Philomena did their best and somehow cobbled together an escape route. Most of the aquemancers made it. They're safe for the moment. But it was risky, a difficult, dangerous process and we don't know if we'll ever get them back. It happened so quickly!"

"What was the rush?"

"The Pyromancer had been investigating aquemancy. He decided, quite suddenly, that it was a danger to his own power. One morning, only three weeks ago, the balloon went up. There were dawn raids, sudden arrests, snap searches. Fortunately, we'd had a couple of hours' warning, and most of the aquemancers managed to get away."

"What about Wincy?"

"Wincy is – out of commission. She was arrested by the Pyromancer…"

"What?" This was dreadful. "I thought you said most of the aquemancers had escaped?"

"Don't worry." Randall cut some bread and began to eat. "Wincy can look after herself."

"But they burn witches!"

"She got away."

"Where is she, then?"

He wouldn't answer her. He took a bottle from a shelf and poured some sour wine for her.

She scowled. "Why won't you tell me? You're treating me like a child, as if I was still little. Why haven't you been pressed, anyway?"

He gestured at the rags he was wearing. "I don't dress like this for fun, Laura."

She saw that there were lines on his face she'd never seen before, that the shadows beneath his eyes were not just dirt.

"I'm sorry, Randall," she said, standing up. She laid a hand on his sleeve. "Will this make things much worse for you? Me being here, I mean?"

He said nothing but she saw the answer in his face.

They'd made everything worse by coming here. Everything.

CHAPTER 4

Conscript

"Let me go!"

"Settle down." The guard's voice was bored.

"You've made a mistake! I've done nothing, I have to let my sister know where I am –"

"Oh, shut up. Put this on." The guard was holding out a yellow and orange tabard to him. A scarlet dragon was embroidered over the chest. The garish colours made Darius's head ache worse. The guard flung the tabard at him. "Here you are. You can let your sister know where you are later. Someone will have told her, anyway. She won't be worrying."

"You don't understand! We came here for the festival…"

"More fool you. There's no festival this year. Not since the Lord Lerris took over. Now, try this."

A bronze helmet followed the tabard, and a sword belt. The scabard was empty. The guard, who was wearing a full-sleeved sparkling white shirt and orange breeches beneath a black tabard, looked as if he was about to go on parade. He was bare-headed, his glossy black hair oiled into a neat braid.

He stood lounging elegantly against the wall as Darius struggled with straps and buttons and belts. At last it was done. Darius picked up the helmet uncertainly. It weighed a ton.

"Put it on," the soldier said.

Darius did as he was told. He peered through the bars of the visor and it felt like being in prison. "Look, I'm no soldier –"

"You are now. You've been pressed, lad. Shut up and make the best of it. It could be worse."

"Worse? How?" Darius subsided on the bench once more, wrestling with the straps to the helmet, which were cutting into his neck.

He'd spent all night alone in a cell, worrying about Laura, alternately shouting and rattling the bars. No one came, no one brought him food.

In the morning someone had pushed a dish of ham and eggs through the bars. There was a hot peppery spice sprinkled over the eggs which he hardly noticed, except it made him sneeze. He'd eaten half of the food before he thought to ask where he was, *why* he was there.

"I'll tell you how it could be worse, my lad." The guard was speaking to him. "You could be on the run. Just in case you get any ideas. They get the dogs out for deserters, you know. We haven't lost a boy since the Lord Lerris took over." The man smiled unpleasantly. His teeth were very white. "You're here for five years' service. Here's your indentures." He waved a sheaf of papers at Darius and flicked them away again before they could be read.

"What?" Darius was enraged. "I'm not a soldier, I'm not even Brican! I was just visiting the city for the festival, with my sister –"

"Tough. That's how it goes. The Earl's building up his forces and anyone on the wander, boy or man, he doesn't much care, gets free board and lodging for five years, courtesy of His Honour's generosity."

"This is ridiculous –"

"Listen, lad." There was a touch, just a touch, of sympathy in the soldier's voice. "There are many worse ways of earning a living, you know. It'll make a man of you, get rid of some of that puppy fat." And with that he turned and left Darius to his thoughts.

A soldier. He'd nagged his father for years about it. He'd always wanted to be there, in uniform, deeds of danger and courage, a way of *proving* himself. His father had medals, had made a name for himself when he was young.

He wanted to do the same. He sat back, gripped by the thought.

Here he was in Bricus, conscripted into the Earl's guard. This was his chance, his way to make his own life, his own career. A country shopkeeper! No way. No way was he going to bury himself in the provinces.

The uniform was made of heavy linen, boldly embroidered with the dragon motif. Darius fingered the rough material with distaste. It was also rather tight under the arms, and the sword belt really needed another hole in it. Darius thought of himself as well-made, although Laura sometimes called him podgy…

Puppy-fat, indeed. But he had to admit that the guard had looked fit, wide-shouldered, narrow-hipped. Slim and strong. A real man's man. And his uniform had been immaculate, sparkling with braid, the seams all perfectly pressed.

Darius wondered whether he'd ever manage to look like that. He traced the outline of the dragon on his chest and knew it was impressive.

Somehow the prospect of five years in the Earl's employ lost a little of its sting.

He was going to be a soldier. His father had been a soldier, it was in his blood. His father had insisted that he and Laura learn –

Laura. What would be happening to her?

They started training later that day. Darius was ordered to run round a field with twenty other young men and then to leap over a succession of wide ditches. Then round the field twice more. The ditches again, followed by high jumping. This went on all morning. After a quick meal of soup and cheese, they were taken to an archway hung with ropes. Everyone had to climb to the top and down again ten times. Then there were exercises, marching round a square while a red-faced sergeant yelled at them.

By the end of it Darius was almost sobbing with exhaustion. His arms were on fire, his legs felt like jelly. The others were not in a much better state. He sneaked a quick look at them as they sat slumped in the refectory, waiting for the supper to be dished out.

Most of them were of a similar age, one or two of them very thin, as if they'd been taken from the streets. There was a bold-looking youth with curly red hair whose language caused some uneasy sniggers. A tall, thin youth with straight black hair and unblinking eyes said little, but managed the rope climbs and runs far ahead of everyone else.

Darius found himself sitting next to him at the wide table. He was almost too tired to lift his spoon to his mouth, but he made the effort to sound friendly. No one else was talking much.

"You done this kind of thing before?" he asked.

"Why?"

"Well, you're good at it."

"I've been practising," the thin dark boy said.

"Did you want to join the guard then?"

"Of course." He'd finished the spicy stew already, was wiping the plate with his bread. His hair lay very flat across the top of his head. He didn't look at Darius.

"I was pressed. I don't belong here."

The other said nothing.

"Why did you want to join, then?" Darius persisted.

"It's a profession. Something worthwhile." The boy glanced at him for the first time.

It encouraged Darius. "My name's Darius," he said, "Darius Brooke." He waited.

"Perrian." There was no indication whether this was a first or second name. Its owner stood up, and his chair grated against the floor. "See you," Perrian said, and left the dining hall.

Darius's bed was in a dormitory with thirty others. A thin line of windows near the ceiling provided the only ventilation. There was a cubicle at one end, a small, inadequate washroom with a highly irregular water supply. The stink of sweat and unwashed bodies was rank and sour. There was a chest beside each bed for clothes, but no one bothered to keep anything private there. All the locks had been broken long ago.

The doors to the dormitory were locked every night. The compound where they exercised was surrounded by barbed wire. Everyone who entered the barracks had to pass through a checkpoint where he was searched and ticked off against a list of permitted personnel.

"How does the Earl ever expect loyalty from soldiers he keeps locked up?" puzzled Darius.

"There'll be a test," said Perrian shortly. "Separating the cannon-fodder from the elite. You wait and see."

"How do you know so much about it?" Darius and Perrian were sitting on a bench outside the refectory a few days later. Inside, a game of dice was causing a lot of noisy argument. Someone was shouting that the dice were loaded, that it wasn't fair and it sounded like there was going to be a fight.

There had been other fights. They all lived too close to each other. Tobacco was always being stolen, girlfriends criticized, toes trodden on or soup spilled. Darius found the reasons trivial, the violence of the fights out of all proportion. Was it going to go on like this? He did his best to avoid trouble, irritably wandering the compound in the evening. He wanted to get on with the job, to learn how to be a soldier.

But underneath it all there was a constant undercurrent of worry. Laura. What was happening to her, how was she managing? There were hazards to being a young girl alone in a big city, he knew. He could hardly bear to think what might be taking place.

There was nothing he could do. There were locks everywhere, roll calls, fences, dogs, guards.

As twins Darius and Laura had done everything together from the day of their birth. They did not look alike, Darius being much more heavily built, with glossy black curling hair. Laura's hair was straight, usually plaited, her figure thin and wiry as a whippet. But she understood what Darius was thinking before he knew it himself, time and time again. She always laughed at his jokes, too, although no one else ever understood them.

And he could always defuse her anger, her flaring rages, before she did something awful. Like the time she'd stayed out overnight in the willow copse.

He worried about what would be happening to her, when he had the time. There'd be trouble, he had no doubt. How could she possibly manage alone in this strange and violent city? If only they could have found Wincy and Randall!

Slavery was common in Bricus, and young girls fetched high prices on the black markets. Even if Laura managed to avoid the slavers, he'd heard that people were murdered for the sake of their hair (Laura's was long, black, thick and beautiful), or sold to aspiring pyromancers for experiments.

He shuddered. That was the worst he could imagine. People frequently lost their lives in pyromantic experiments. Occasionally you'd see beggars on the streets with charred stumps of limbs, their eyes burned out by the bright flaring of magical fires.

"What's the matter?" Franklin, one of the street boys, had come up to the bench where Darius and Perrian were sitting. He was undersized, pale and thin, someone who failed over and over at the exercises. He had knock-knees and pigeon-toes. His legs were purple with the bruises he had received in the course of the day.

"Nothing." Even after only a few days, Darius knew better than to admit weakness in the camp.

"Get lost." Perrian barely bothered to look at Franklin.

"I only—"

"There is nothing, not one thing you could say that could possibly be of interest to us."

Darius glanced at Perrian in surprise. This was by far the longest speech he'd ever heard him make.

Franklin flushed, and turned away.

"What have you got against him?" Darius asked.

Perrian shrugged. "He's a loser. A street-kid, a no-hoper. You don't need people like that."

"What do you mean?"

Perrian turned to face him. "You still haven't got it, have you? What this is about?"

"We're being trained for the guard."

"Yes, but some will be officers, and some will not. You are officer material, as I am, and the street boys are not. It's simple enough."

"He could be clever. How can anyone know?"

"If he was clever, he wouldn't be on the streets. Anyway, the test will be held soon."

"What test? How do you know so much about this?"

Perrian stood up. "My father is in the Earl's personal guard. He told me. I know how every-thing works here." He leaned forward suddenly. "And I'll tell you something else. The test is in two parts. When you come to the second, whatever you do, don't hold back. Breathe in the smoke. A good deep breath. It shows trust and loyalty. It's the one sure way to get into the Earl's own Guard."

"What?" It sounded bizarre.

"You heard. Breathe in the smoke as if it were the sweetest, freshest air in the world."

"Why?"

"You'll see. Later."

"Why are you being so mysterious about this?"

"Because although you're fit and straight and not stupid, I don't know whether we can trust you."

Darius's jaw dropped. What did Perrian mean by "we"? He didn't understand any of this.

"Anyway," said Perrian. "You brush your teeth and don't snore." A gleam in his dark eyes. Darius couldn't decide whether it was humour or not. "You're in with a chance. And if I've got to share with anyone, I'd rather it was you than any of the others."

CHAPTER 5

Testing Time

That night Darius couldn't sleep. Talking to Perrian had suddenly brought home to him that he had no way out of this. He was going to be a soldier, possibly an officer, and although this was something he'd always wanted, he might not be free to see Laura again for years.

He hadn't been able to eat much that evening with the worry of it. He kept thinking of his twin, wondering how she was. He was kicking himself for bringing her to Bricus.

He forgot that it hadn't been his decision. Because he was the bigger twin, and technically the older (by ten minutes), he was used to thinking of himself as the wiser, the more dominant of the two.

But actually, Laura had initiated most of their

adventures. It had been Laura who had first suggested that the Brican festival might be fun. He felt slightly cheered, remembering that Laura was really quite competent, inventive even, for a girl.

Well, she was his twin. It stood to reason that she'd be able to look after herself. She'd had his example, all those years.

But still the nagging memory of those burned beggars would not leave his mind.

Eventually, he threw back the covers and crept to the end of the dormitory, where Perrian slept, and put his hand out to wake the sleeping form.

His fingers sank into softness. The bed was empty, the sleeping figure nothing more than a pillow turned sideways. He stood there for a moment, quite still, and then went quickly to the door.

It was locked as usual. He made a quick check, looking into the washing cubicle, kneeling down and peering under the ranks of beds. There was no sign of Perrian anywhere in the dormitory and yet the door was locked.

He couldn't understand it. And then he realized that he was being watched, that someone was following his movements.

Franklin was sitting up in bed, calmly considering him. "And just what do you think you're up to?" he asked. "Looking for pickings?"

"What? No, of course not —"

"You happen to like wandering round in the dead of night? If you're going to make a career of it, I think you'd better learn to be rather quieter on your feet. Or are you a spy or something?"

"No – I –"

Other people had been woken by their voices. There was a clamour of shouting and accusations.

"What's he doing?"

"Thief!"

"Who're you to talk?"

"Shut up! It's late!"

"Filthy toe-rag –"

Someone threw a boot at Darius. He scuttled back to the bed and pulled the covers over him.

No one else had noticed that Perrian wasn't there.

Next day there was no chance to talk to Perrian. They were put through a gruelling series of boxing bouts and not once did he find himself anywhere near the tall thin youth.

After supper, Franklin came looking for him. "What were you doing last night?" he asked tiredly. There were great blisters on his palms from digging ditches. He'd had to miss the midday meal as a punishment for failing to get any points at all during the first round of fights. They'd set him to digging useless trenches, and he was staggering with exhaustion.

There was something about him that made Darius want to confide. Franklin was so unthreatening, so uncompetitive.

"I couldn't sleep," he muttered. "I wanted to talk to someone."

"Who were you looking for?" Franklin was still steadily watching him and for the first time Darius noticed how thoughtful his eyes were.

"Perrian," said Darius softly. "He seems to know what's going on."

Franklin took his time answering. He sat down next to Darius on a bench and turned his hands palm up to the cooling breeze. "You discovered he wasn't there," he said and it wasn't a question.

"How could he have got out?" Darius almost shouted. "The door was locked, I checked it. How did he manage to get away?"

There was another pause. Then Franklin said, "I don't know. I never see what happens. But he hardly ever spends the whole night in the dormitory."

"Well, where does he go? Has he got a key?" And then Darius remembered what Perrian had said, that his father was in the Earl's private Guard. All at once he regretted talking to Franklin. "Anyway, it doesn't matter what Perrian does," he said. "I've got other things to worry about."

"Tell Uncle Franklin."

Darius laughed. Franklin was at least six inches

shorter than he, with pale wispy hair blowing across his thin face. He looked absurdly young, and yet there was something very knowing in his eyes. You didn't live on the streets of Bricus for a lifetime and end up an innocent, Darius realized. He said, "Is it true that the pyromancers use people off the streets for experiments?"

Franklin nodded. "If they're down and out, and have no friends." He looked sharply at Darius. "Why, have you lost someone?"

"My sister," he said bleakly. "We came to Bricus together. I don't know what happened to her when I was pressed."

"How old is she?" asked Franklin, seriously.

"The same as me. We're twins," he said.

"Does she look like you?"

"Not really. She's got all this long dark hair, and she's much thinner... What's the matter?" he shouted, seeing the closed expression on Franklin's face.

"If she's quick on her feet, and not silly..." He stopped.

"God, I wish we'd never come!" Darius leaned his head in his hands.

"Bricus isn't a good place these days," said Franklin. "Things have changed. It's hard to believe it. This time six months ago, everything was totally different. But then nowhere's good if you're on your own."

"What about the slavers? What about the hair thieves?"

Franklin looked at him sadly. "They're all out there, looking for trade. But there's nothing you can do to help your sister now. Nothing at all."

"God, I'd do anything to get out of here!" he shouted.

"Anything?" said Perrian, coming up behind him. "Do you mean that, Darius?"

"Yes!"

"Well, then, work hard. Get promoted. Get into the Earl's Guard. You'll have privileges then, you'll be able to do whatever you want. You'll have more freedom and prestige than you'll know what to do with."

"Are you sure?"

"Of course. Why do you think I'm here?"

Darius shrugged with frustration. Promotion seemed a long way off, the Earl's Guard an impossible dream.

The tests took place next day. All morning they were marched up and down, back and forth through the compound. There were kit inspections, weapons drill and, most gruelling of all, a series of athletic trials. There were wrestling and boxing matches, fencing contests, knife-handling tournaments. Officers in the Earl's insignia watched everything, inscrutable behind their visored helmets.

By sunset, Darius was on his knees. But that wasn't the end of it. After supper they were taken across the quadrangle to a hall in the Earl's palace and sat at desks in long rows and handed pencils.

Looking round, it became clear to Darius that a fair proportion of his fellow conscripts did not know what a pencil was. Some distance behind him he saw Franklin squint at it, holding it up to the light, turning it between finger and thumb. Darius mimed to him writing, scribbling in the air, but this only increased Franklin's air of mystification. What use was it? Franklin couldn't even read. Darius felt a fool for not realizing.

And then somebody banged a staff on the dais at one end of the hall. Darius hadn't seen him come in.

The figure on the dais dominated the hall. He was dressed in long golden robes that trailed over the floor around him. Great pools of golden fabric sparkled in the torchlight, cascading down over the steps to the dais. The material was embroidered with the usual scarlet dragon design.

The man's face was hidden. Like certain of the officers in the Earl's Guard, he wore a visored helmet over his face, although this was rather more elaborate than the ones worn by the ordinary soldiers. The sunburst design was studded with jewels, weighted with gold and amber.

The hall had fallen silent before the Pyromancer.

After a pause, a pause which seemed to go on for just that bit too long, so that Darius began to feel rather uncomfortable, the Pyromancer motioned one of the guards forward to read from a scroll. The man's voice was dry and monotonous and Darius, seated half-way up the hall, could hardly hear what he said. Others further back would have no chance.

"Attention. You have today completed the physical aspect of your trial. There will be other, more subtle, assessments, but we are concerned now with the quality of your minds.

"We are about to distribute your examination papers. You are to remain silent at all times. Any attempt to view anyone else's paper will be regarded as cheating and the candidate disqualified. You will have the time it takes for the oil in the bronzed bowl to burn to complete the questions on the paper. No questions are allowed."

There was a clamour at the back because no one had heard. The guard stood back. The noise increased until the figure in the visor banged his staff sharply on the floor. "Silence!" They heard the Pyromancer's voice for the first time. The word hissed through the air like acid. The noise died down.

The Pyromancer turned to a bowl supported by a stand on the side of the dais. He clapped his hand once over the bowl, and flame shot up into the air. There was a sweet, sickly scent filling the hall. It reminded Darius of the peppery spice that was sprinkled over all their food.

Was it a drug? The unwelcome suspicion filtered into Darius's mind, quickly to be dismissed. He was too anxious to do well in this examination. He had to win his promotion to the Earl's Guard.

As soon as the bowl was lit, slaves began to move up and down the aisles, laying pieces of paper face down in front of each candidate.

"You may begin," said someone. The Pyromancer was standing by the golden bowl, concentrating on something in its burning centre. Smoke twined round the golden figure.

Holding his breath, Darius turned the paper over.

Immediately he was filled with relief. It was the kind of test he had done a hundred times at home already. He was well used to the questions which ran, Put the next in sequence in the blank square. Which is the odd one out? Which shape fits here? What is the connection? etc., etc.

None of them was particularly difficult. He zipped through the questions as quickly as he could, vowing to go back to complete any he'd missed.

But before he did so, he looked back. The back of the room was in disarray. Everyone was quite silent, but no one was working. Some were asleep, some picked their noses, other had their feet up on the desks, tilting their chairs back recklessly. He saw Franklin holding his head in his hands, staring hopelessly at the paper. Some folded their papers into the shape of paper darts and white missiles skimmed through the air.

It seemed to him that the roughest types, the street boys and gutterlings, were seated right at the back. They were also, he thought grimly, the ones who couldn't read.

What was the purpose of putting them through something like this? It seemed ridiculous to him. He found himself speculating on what would happen in the second part of the test.

At last the flames in the bowl died down, and the Pyromancer lifted his mask from the smoke, held up his staff and banged it on the floor. Everyone looked up. The slaves darted forward to collect the papers, and the Pyromancer raised his hands over the shiny brass bowl. Darius noticed for the first time that there was something glinting round his neck beneath the helmet, a chain of office or locket of some kind.

He remembered what he knew of Pyromancers. They carried their magic with them in bottles, he had heard somewhere. Potions, familiar spirits, all sorts of enchantments... Some people held that they kept monsters imprisoned in bottles, like the genii of old legends.

The man handed the staff to one of the slaves and raised his hands to unclasp the chain round his neck. From a locket he took something Darius couldn't make out, and threw it into the smoking remains in the bowl.

Immediately flames soared, almost reaching to the ceiling above them. This scent was pungent, a much stronger concentration of that already familiar smell. It had a sulphurous edge to it, reeking through the air so that the men in the front rows began to cough and clear their throats.

The Pyromancer showed no discomfort. His acolyte stepped forward. "One by one you are to approach the dais and let the sacred smoke embrace you," he said. "Your fates are to be decided by the Spirit of the Fire."

Row by row the conscripts filed up to the dais and the smoke wafted towards them. It wreathed around them, hiding them from sight until, without exception, they all staggered blindly out of its grip, their eyes and noses running. When it came to Darius's turn he stood very still, watching carefully as the blanket of smoke began to twirl towards him. At the very last moment, as it blanketed over all his face, he took a deep breath, as Perrian had instructed.

Immediately he felt that the top of his head had blown off. Clear showers of scarlet spice ran through his sinuses, blasting through his brain, blasting away his thoughts and memories.

It wasn't pleasant, but then neither did it hurt. It felt as if he was beginning to think properly for the first time. He had no intention of being like the other miserable, choking conscripts. He was going to be different, he was going to be chosen for something special.

A soldier in the Earl's own Guard. He stepped out of the smoke and went down the steps again. He was aware of the Pyromancer's hidden eyes following him out of the hall. As he waited in the ranks for everyone to emerge Darius caught Perrian's arm.

His friend winked at him. They stood straight and tall, side by side in the cooling evening, and waited for their summons.

CHAPTER 6

Quinland

"Get it over with." Laura held the scissors out to Randall. Without a word, he took a handful of thick black hair and cut it off.

She watched the glossy locks fall to the floor with resignation. She was already wearing ragged breeches and a filthy, fraying shirt Randall had found in a bag of jumble sale scraps. He'd let her keep her own shoes, but insisted that she scuff them against the wall and stain them with earth from the garden.

He was ruthless with her hair. Only an inch or two of spiky tufts remained. "What are you going to do with it?" she asked, watching him sweep it all up.

He stuffed it into a bag. "If things get bad, we'll sell it," he said. "Or perhaps we can make you a wig when this is all over."

Her mouth dropped. "A *wig*?"

"Or you can wait until it grows back." He shrugged. "You insisted on coming, Laura. If you'd done as your parents had wanted you'd be tucked up at home right now, instead of losing all your glory in a dusty heap on the floor."

"I told you before," she said. "Darius wanted to come." (*So did I,* she said to herself. *I made Darius come. I knew something was wrong, I knew Wincy was in trouble…*) "Darius was determined to get to the festival and we always stay together, we're never apart."

"I know." He sounded exasperated. "But neither of you had any idea what the risks are."

"Well, you've told me now. All about the Earl and his wife and the new Pyromancer and the slavers and thieves and murderers! I know all that—"

"You know it intellectually. You have no actual idea what it's like to live under cover here."

"Well, I'll soon find out, then, won't I?" She raised her chin at him. "Give me those." She took the scissors from him and attempted to even up the mess he'd made.

"I'm only letting you stay here because travelling is also unsafe for a girl on her own, and

I cannot possibly leave Bricus to take you home right now."

"I think you've got some explaining to do." She could hardly believe that she was saying these things, challenging her handsome older cousin like this. "Where have all the water-witches gone? Why aren't they fighting back?"

"That's what all this is about. We need to find them as quickly as possible and it's so difficult. It's probably best that you don't get too involved."

"Why? Are you afraid I'll give you away?" This was awful. She could feel her temper rising. "I think you might trust me, Randall!"

He put his hands on her shoulders. "I do trust you, Laura. But you have never been in the power of a pyromancer, have you? Have you even seen one at work? Seen a firefly in action? I would rather keep you well clear of such sights, Laura. And the less you know, the less likely you are to find yourself in trouble."

"Come on, Randall." She looked straight at him. "We came to Bricus knowing nothing at all and immediately found ourselves in this mess. Ignorance is no protection."

"Bravo!" Another voice.

Laura spun round. There was a man standing in the corner of the room behind her. She gasped. No one had come in, the door had not opened and she was sure that he had not been there before.

"What – ? Who are you?" she stammered, taking a step backwards.

"Really, Quinland, why must you always show off?" Randall sounded irritated. "Laura, this is a friend of mine and Wincy's. You can call him Quinland. Laura's my cousin, Quin. She and her brother thought they were coming for a jolly stay during the festival."

The man held out his hand to Laura but she hung back. "I don't understand. Where did you come from? How did you get in here?"

He smiled at her. He was a lot older than Randall, at least forty. He wore beggar's clothes, just like she and Randall, and there was an empty hessian bag over his shoulder. His hair was a nondescript light brown, his face unremarkable, apart from dark eyes snapping with amusement. He was slight, quite a bit shorter than Randall.

She frowned.

"I came down the drainpipe," he said and she had no idea whether he was being serious or not. In the corner behind him Laura saw some old lead piping leading from the ceiling to the drain in the floor. A few drops of water still clung to the grating over the drain.

"Don't look so surprised, Laura," said Randall. "You've heard of pyromancy, haven't you? Well, Quinland is an aquemancer, one who elected to stay behind. But he has some unusual skills, even for an aquemancer..."

She stared. They had to be joking. People, magicians or not, did not squeeze themselves down drainpipes.

Quinland said, "Enough of that, if you please, Randall, stop teasing the girl. Laura, I've been here all the time. I fell asleep over there." He pointed to a dark corner among the boxes. "There's nothing at all magical about it. I am of course delighted to meet you, and some other day you must explain to me exactly why you thought Bricus a suitable place for a holiday, but now I need to talk to Randall. In private."

"You said 'Bravo'," she said slyly. "I said that ignorance is no protection, and you cheered."

"Heaven preserve me from clever women!" Quinland raised an eyebrow at Randall. "I suppose we deserved that. What do you think, Randall?"

Randall sighed, and pulled up another chair to the table. "She's going to be here for some time. Perhaps we ought to explain."

And so they did.

They told her about the arrival of the Pyromancer in Bricus. "Everything started to go wrong then," said Quinland. "Up to that point, we thought that at long last the aquemancers were going to be accepted by Brican society. Aquemancy had always been viewed with suspicion in the past. But things were changing. Why, Marrin, the Earl of Bricus and a notable pyromancer himself, had even married Philomena, an aquemancer of extraordinary power. She's one of the weather-witches, a most unusual and highly esteemed skill."

"A weather-witch? What do they do, make it rain?"

"That's it," said Randall. "A skill beyond price in these latitudes. This is why there's a drought now... You may have noticed."

Laura nodded.

"Well, Philomena and Wincy worked together to regulate the weather around Bricus. Usually, there's too much rain in the winter and none in the summer. Their job was to make it more equitable."

"I can remember my mother being over the moon about Philomena marrying the Earl of Bricus," Laura said. "She and Wincy knew Philomena when they were children."

"Well, we all thought that aquemancy would at last come in from the cold," Quinland continued. "But then old Lord Renfrew, the Pyromancer who had blessed the marriage between Marrin and Philomena, died. And after his death a letter was found in his belongings appointing Lerris as his successor.

"It was accepted without question. Although no one in Bricus had ever met Lerris before, his reputation was well known. Lerris was famous throughout Rustria and the Southern states. He was invited to the city and after a brief interview with the Earl, was appointed Lord High Pyromancer."

"Within a month, he'd outlawed public displays of aquemancy," said Randall grimly. "And at the same time, Marrin and Philomena's marriage began to go wrong. Seriously wrong. Marrin began to suspect that Philomena was unfaithful: he found letters, a man's handkerchief; she smelled of sandalwood. There were unexplained absences (she was actually meeting the Council of Aquemancers, trying to work out what to do). She received bouquets from unknown admirers, anonymous poems were discovered in her glove drawer, it all looked suspicious."

Quinland said, "We suspect this is Lerris's doing. That was Wincy's theory, anyway. She came to see us, three weeks ago. Just before the clampdown. She said that Marrin had changed out of all recognition. It was as if he was possessed, she said. She was disturbed, and I've never seen Wincy upset like that before."

And Laura remembered her cousin's face, seen in that moonlit bottle, so serious, so stressed. She shivered.

"Wincy said that she and Philomena had been working on a method of escape. She showed me what to do, and swore it would only be used as a desperate measure. Within the week, we were using it. The Earl banned water-witches from the city on pain of death by firefly. And Lerris sent out the Guard to search the city and they found—"

"No one." Randall spoke with satisfaction. "We were in time. They'd all gone, every one of them. Quin and I are the only aquemancers left."

"But what happened to Wincy?" asked Laura.

"She was captured by the Pyromancer and sentenced to execution by firefly. But she got away and no one has seen her since. She's lying low somewhere, and I don't mind admitting that I'm worried –" He flashed a glance at Quinland. "We're both worried. She may have been injured escaping from the execution. We don't even really know if she's still alive. And if the Pyromancer's beginning to learn aquemancy he'll be able to get at the aquemancers anyway. We'll never see Wincy again."

Quinland was looking at his hands, his face shadowed so that Laura could not see his expression.

"We don't know where Philomena is either. Her father, Lord Dulchimer, is missing too. We spend our time looking."

"Where do you look?" asked Laura. "Where are they hiding?"

"Ah, now, that's the difficulty in all this. The aquemancers are unreachable in ordinary terms. It's the most difficult and long-winded of processes. There is no way to bring the water-witches back without a huge amount of hard work and a considerable degree of luck."

"Why? How does it work?"

"We need Wincy or the Countess. They're the only ones who know the truth of it, apart from Quin. There was no time to reach anyone else."

"Where did they go?" Laura repeated. She still didn't understand.

Quinland and Randall exchanged glances. "Into the dreaming," said Quinland at last. "It's difficult to explain."

Laura wanted to ask more but Quinland was on his feet now, flinging himself up and down the cramped room, as if he had too much energy to sit still. "Surely, *surely* she would have made some effort to contact us? She must know we'd be frantic!"

And then Randall explained. "Laura – Quinland and Wincy are engaged to be married, you see. He's like one of the family."

It made sense. Quinland's anxiety and impatience fell into place.

"I'm so sorry, Quinland," said Laura. "I've lost

someone too. I know how you must be feeling."

"Darius will be all right," said Randall sharply. Briefly he explained to Quinland who Darius was. "You really must believe me, Laura. No harm will come to Darius so long as he keeps his wits about him and toes the line."

"What if he mentions Wincy's name?" she said. The two men looked at her.

"She's our cousin. We've got Alderwood as a middle name. What if he says who we are?" she was almost shouting.

Randall took a deep breath. "Then the Earl will have an Alderwood hostage. A lever to use against us," he said calmly. "We can only hope that Darius keeps his mouth shut."

"He won't," said Laura. "He always blabs, he can never keep a secret, he's just a great stupid chatterbox." She burst into tears.

CHAPTER 7

City Life

Later, when Laura was calmer, Quinland said goodbye to them and left Randall's hideaway through the garden shed trapdoor. He took with him the sack of bottles, handling them with great care.

"Returning the empties?" Laura asked as Randall lifted the sack up to Quinland.

His brown face, wise like a monkey's, peered down at her. "Sort of," he said. "If you really want to help us find Wincy – I mean really help – pick up any bottles you find, bottles with something in them. Doesn't matter what it is. Bring them to me."

"Why do you want...?" she began, but he'd gone. She looked at Randall.

"No," he said, before she'd even started. "Don't even ask. It sounds ridiculous but it's part of getting the other aquemancers back. I do it too. The ones Quinland took with him were bottles I'd collected yesterday."

"Where does he live?" she asked.

"Here and there. He has a house over near the market but I never know exactly where he is. But somehow he's always around whenever I want him."

"How long have you known—"

He shook his head. "Enough questions, Laura. We've got work to do. Now, let's have a look at you." He picked up a candlestick from the table and peered closely at her face. "More dirt," he said briefly. "As we go through the garden rub your hands in the soil and smear your face. One thing –" He suddenly grinned. "I'd rather try to pass you off as a street urchin than that great galumphing twin of yours. No one would ever believe he'd had to scavenge for food."

"Poor Darius."

She began to feel miserable again and quickly changed the subject. "What work *do* you do?" She envisaged him as a street entertainer, juggling or fire-eating. It was easier to imagine than Randall as a thief or beggar, elegant dignified Randall, the star of all her childhood crushes. But it was strange, she thought, how quickly she'd got used to him dressed in filthy rags. It made him more accessible somehow, made him look more friendly and ordinary. She no longer felt breathless when he looked at her, as she had at home. Or had she just grown up since they'd last met?

With a shock she suddenly realized what he was holding out to her.

A knife, the blade as long as her hand, gleaming silvery sharp in the candlelight.

"Do you know how to use this?" Randall asked.

She nodded. Her father had always insisted that she should be able to defend herself, even though they lived in a quiet country village. He'd been an instructor in the army before retiring to the country, and knew how to teach... She'd complained at the lessons at first but soon came to enjoy them. She was lightning quick on her feet and even though her reach was so much shorter than Darius's, often managed to disarm him.

They'd practised using knives made of wood. This was steel, sharp enough to slice hair. Randall gave her a sheath for it and showed her how to tape it along her left forearm.

Then he helped her up through the trapdoor and out into the garden.

It was daylight. Laura had rather lost track of time and stood in the sun for a moment blinking in the brightness. Outside the shed the garden was full of chrysanthemums and asters, late roses and geraniums, all still in bloom, a last desperate flowering against the ferocious late summer heat. Nasturtiums tangled over the path. Dutifully she bent down and scooped up some earth to rub into her face. The scent of geraniums reminded her of home.

"Come on," said Randall, opening the gate. "I want you to get to know Bricus as soon as you can. Not the Bricus the visitors and well-off know, the safe clean orderly ways of the city, but the other Bricus, where my friends live. I want to show you the bolt holes, the short-cuts and alleys. There are safe houses too, where you can go for shelter at any time. A fair number of Brican citizens are sympathetic to our cause, and are willing to help out. I need to introduce you to them."

They were out in Silver Street now, where the rubbish still clung to the steps in noxious heaps. Flies were buzzing everywhere. Laura saw a dark shape move amongst the debris and took it for a cat. Only when it ran, suddenly disappearing under a door trailing a long scaly tail after it, did she realize that it was a rat.

"Where are we going?"

"To find some friends. People who will help you. You need to know it all, Laura, if this is going to work."

"Or else?"

"Or else I lock you in under the garden shed. I can't run any risks with you, my uncle and aunt would never forgive me." He glanced sideways at her to see how she was taking it. "OK, Laura?"

She hated it when he acted like her parents. "Lead the way, Dally," she said, greatly daring. She knew it would irritate him.

"*What?* What did you call me?"

"Dally. That's what we nicknamed you when we were little. Dally and Winc, that's who you were." She grinned at him, but he was aloof.

"I won't tell you what your nicknames were," he said unkindly.

"I know," she said. "You and Wincy called us the Twinlings. We overheard you once. We rather liked it, we were never offended."

"Well, you can call me Dally, if you like. I don't mind either."

But she knew she wouldn't. Her cousin Randall had lost his sense of humour since his last visit to the country two years ago. She wasn't at all sure that she liked it.

The Bricus Randall knew intrigued Laura. It was a place of concealed exits and entrances, of doorways that looked like walls, of passages that led nowhere and stairs where you least expected them.

The secret was in the illusions. No magic was

involved in this. But doors were disguised by painted bricks so that they were indistinguishable from walls. Stairs disappeared in the play of light and shade between wrought-iron pillars. Curtains of ivy hung down over other walk-ways. Seeming dead ends proved to have ropes looped behind drainpipes.

"You may need to run," said Randall plainly, "and you won't have time to look for disguised doorways then. You'll have to learn each of these routes, Laura, and hope you'll never need them." He paused and she wondered what he was going to say next. "And something else," he said eventually. "If you ever find yourself pursued by a pyromancer, with or without a firefly, make for water. Any water, although it's getting difficult these days. The river's almost dried up and they've cut off practically all the town's fountains and drained the ornamental ponds. It's the Pyromancer's policy. And we're in the dry season now, we'll be lucky if it rains. But find some water – even a few drops will help – and a firefly won't touch you. They can't bear it."

Over the next few days Laura followed him round the city and every now and then he tested her, patiently taking her back over the routes she'd forgotten or confused. They returned to the garden shed each evening, carrying bags of bottles they'd collected during the day. Sometimes

Quinland came to take them, sometimes Randall went out again. Often, she fell asleep before he returned. They didn't dare cook there, but there was plenty of cheap food available from street vendors.

Gradually, Randall introduced her to his friends. It wasn't planned. Randall and Laura were wandering through the narrow alleys near the river, when they came across two street urchins rooting through a pile of rubbish near some dustbins.

They were black-haired and brown-skinned, thin as rakes, and dressed in rags, like she was. Both of them wore battered old hats with wavy brims as a protection against the fierce heat of the sun. They were gathering bottles, collecting them in a sack. They looked up as Randall approached, saying nothing.

"Laura, this is Max and Nina," said Randall. "Friends of Quinland and Wincy. They're dab hands at the paintwork." He looked at her speculatively. "What are you like as an artist, Laura?"

"Hopeless." She wrinkled her nose. "I drew cats which looked like horses and horses that looked like rabbits. Useless."

"Ahh. Well, never mind. You can still look for bottles."

All the while this was going on Max and Nina

were staring at her, somewhat disdainfully, Laura thought. She wondered if they were related, both with dark eyes and straight noses, the same cool gaze.

She scowled at them and then wondered at her own courage. Usually she left it to Darius to make the running with strangers.

Randall hadn't noticed. He said, "Would you mind looking out for Laura for a couple of hours? She's not been here long and doesn't really know the ropes yet. I'm afraid there's someone I have to go and see –" And before anyone could say anything, he'd disappeared off down one of the alleys.

"Randall?" She almost ran after him. She was aware of being watched. Reluctantly she turned to face Max and Nina.

Max was lounging against the wall, his battered straw hat tilted forward so that she couldn't see his eyes.

"Well," he said at last, "I suppose it's not your fault." It was grudging, to say the least, although there was something she liked about his voice. A colouring of humour, a touch of warmth.

Laura sighed. "I'm sorry," she said. "I had no idea he was going to do that."

"It's not your fault," said Max. He grinned at her and was immediately transformed. His teeth were very white against his dark skin.

Nina hefted the sack of bottles over her shoulder. It looked too heavy for her. "Randall's always so secretive!" she grumbled. "He's always dumping us in it and then wafting off." She smiled too and Laura was irresistibly reminded of a small rodent, a mouse or vole, with sharp, bright eyes. "Don't see why I should carry all these. Ah, there we are." She picked up a piece of old hemp sacking and tied the ends together so that it formed a bag. "Here, you take some of the bottles."

They were dividing them out when Max, who had walked to the end of the road, whistled, a loud piercing noise.

"Quick!" Nina hurriedly jammed the rest of the bottles into Laura's sack and set off in the opposite direction. Max had already caught up with her.

"What...?" Laura stumbled after them.

"Soldiers," said Max shortly. Already they could hear the tread of running feet behind them.

They were tearing down one of the alleys, opening a door as they passed so that it looked as if they'd gone that way.

Then on, to a dead end.

Laura didn't recognize it from her explorations with Randall. She had no idea whether there was a secret exit concealed there amongst the bricks and stones.

It looked like a wall, unpainted, unadorned

with greenery of any description.

There were uniformed men now at the mouth of the alley. They were wearing the visored helmets and scarlet tabards of the Earl's Guard.

One of them was shouting. "Halt! You are under arrest!"

They'd reached the end. Laura was out of breath, a painful stitch in her side. The wall was over twenty feet high, sheer, without hand or footholds.

"What shall we do?" she wailed.

Max had taken one of the bottles from Nina's sack. He glanced at it quickly, then tore out the stopper with his teeth.

He threw the bottle to the ground. It smashed. Immediately a thick green vapour emerged and enveloped them. Nina went right up to the wall and leaned both hands hard against one of the blocks of stone.

It swung silently to one side as if it were on a hinge, leaving a narrow opening. Straight away Nina scrambled up into it, pushing her sack of bottles in front of her.

Laura didn't hesitate. She dived after Nina as if fireflies were after her and was only dimly conscious that Max was right behind her.

Her way was suddenly blocked by Nina's sack of bottles.

"Careful!" a voice said from somewhere below

her. Too far below. Laura found herself looking down over a drop of some ten feet.

"Lower the sack gently," said Nina and Laura leaned over, letting it drop into Nina's upstretched hands.

Then she lowered herself over the edge and jumped the remaining distance.

A second later and Max was at her side.

"Come on," said Nina. "They'll try to cut us off."

They kept running, dodging through passages and upstairs and across roofs and down again.

And then it happened. A soldier suddenly stepped out of a doorway and caught Laura's collar.

"Here, you little vandal! Where do you think you're off to?"

Max and Nina were far ahead. She caught a glimpse of Max's face, his dark eyes flashing with fury.

She wriggled and tore at the man's hands, trying to dislodge his grip.

He was shouting. "This way! I've got one of them!"

Laura kicked his shins. He cursed, but didn't budge. And then it came to her. She didn't know if it would work for her but she could at least try.

She stopped struggling and dug her hand into the sack of bottles, grabbing one at random.

With force, before the man realized what she was doing, she threw it to the ground. It smashed against the cobbles, but instead of thick green vapour, there was a terrible noise, a scream so bloodcurdling that the soldier's hand dropped nervelessly from her collar.

The sound lashed like a flail around them, screeching through the upper registers. Laura put her own hands over her ears, unable to bear the banshee scream echoing off the stone walls around them.

Someone shook her shoulder. She looked with streaming eyes into Max's stormy face. Nina was there too, gathering up the remaining bottles. She looked drawn and frantic. Still the dreadful wailing went on. The air around them was tinged red, blood-stained she thought at first, but then the colour brightened and became fiery, coloured like flames... But the sound went on. It was an expression of agony, of appalling pain, cut through with something horrible, something malevolent, almost evil. The sound seemed sharper than knives, spiky, vicious.

She saw the stones under her feet glistening but it wasn't glass. She didn't understand where the water had come from, but this was the least of her worries.

Other soldiers had reached the junction at the end of the road. And then Laura was hustled into a doorway, a concealed entrance behind some dustbins, and the door slammed shut behind them.

For a moment Laura, Max and Nina crouched there against the door, listening hard. The sound was dying away, and with it the tread of footsteps.

"Where have they gone?" Laura whispered, but no one answered her.

Then: "You criminal fool," said Max to Laura. "Do you know what you've done?"

"No!" she cried. "What was it, what was that noise?"

"A water-witch, dying," Max said tonelessly. "It might even have been Wincy. You could have killed her. You've certainly killed someone."

"Wincy? How? Surely not!" Yet a terrible cold fist clenched in her stomach, a cold tension that made her want to weep.

"Don't you know anything? Anything at all?"

"No," she said humbly. "Nothing."

For a moment he was silent. Then he shook his head in disbelief. "Didn't Randall tell you? What was he doing, letting you loose in the city, gathering bottles, not *knowing*?"

"I think he was going to tell me. Or Quinland was."

"They'll have been worried about security," said Nina plainly. "The more people who know, the more risky it is."

"I'm *family*!" said Laura, very upset. "I'd never

betray them. I'm sure they were going to tell me, but I've only been here a few days." She sounded revoltingly pathetic, even to herself.

"Well, listen then." He spoke with controlled savagery. "It's a technique developed by Wincy and the Countess, very recent, very new. A water-witch – a male or female aquemancer – as a last resort, can transform into a different level of reality. Another dimension, if you like. They say it feels like dreaming. The point is that they physically disappear, become dissipated. Weather-witches tend to use the wind, clouds, storms... It's incredibly dangerous and not all of them make it back. But they all leave something behind, a few drops of water. This is their only way of getting back into this reality. It's their link, their life-line with this world..."

"Drops of water?" This all sounded quite mad.

"Why not? Think about it: after all, we are mostly made of water. Each drop carries the imprint, the memory of the whole. It's not so far-fetched. They can direct the water enough to move it to a hiding place, a bottle or vessel of some kind. A bottle is best, though it can be a dish or a pot or anything. But it's risky, almost suicidal. If the water is spilt, then they're left there, moaning in the wind, crying with the rain. *That's* why we collect bottles. *That's* why we're so careful with them –"

"But you smashed one! And that fog came up –"

"That was something else, a defensive trick Quinland showed us."

"Well, how was I to know? No one told me, you never gave me a chance!"

"You should have waited, you—"

"Stop it, Max!" Nina spoke for the first time. "Listen to her. It's not her fault if no one tells her what's at risk…"

Laura took a deep breath. "But Wincy… Could that really have been Wincy?"

"In theory, yes." Max looked her straight in the eye. She thought how intense he was, how passionate. "But don't worry. I don't think that was Wincy. She would be more in control than that poor soul was. She'd never have let go screaming."

"Then what was it?" Laura hardly dared look at him.

"I don't know. Hundreds of aquemancers have had to go into hiding recently and not all of them are white witches. I felt something horrible in that one, something evil. It may even have been for the best…"

It was some comfort. But not much.

CHAPTER 8

The Trial

The results of the tests were announced next day. As Darius expected, the street boys and guttersnipes were all allocated to the ranks. Only a few of the others were singled out for special training, Darius and Perrian among them.

Darius watched Franklin being marched away to the barracks with some sympathy. He'd make a hopeless soldier, he was nowhere near strong enough to hold his own among that collection of meat-heads.

Darius himself, together with Perrian and six or seven others, was led into the quadrangle which separated the palace from the barracks. They were kept waiting there in the bright sunlight until their heads began to ache. Around them the stone colonnades looked cool and shady.

In the distance Darius saw the dazzle from the glass towers from the north wing of the palace. It reminded him of nothing so much as a vast greenhouse. Except there was no sign of any green, growing thing there. The slanted glass roofs were sparkling bright. Darius wondered who ever kept them clean.

It was a relief when one of the Earl's own courtiers came to fetch them. The man's face was hidden behind one of the visored helmets. He was dressed in flowing silks in flame colours, with the plain black tabard embroidered with a scarlet dragon. The man led them under the colonnades into stifling halls, down brilliant corridors and up sweeping stairways. The palace was on a massive scale, and Darius very soon lost his sense of direction.

Eventually, they were lined up in one of the antechambers in the north wing.

This was a bleached and baking glasshouse, identical to a dozen others they had passed through. The sun burned down through the glass roof. As if it were not already hot enough, a brazier heaped with red-hot coals stood in the centre of the marble floor.

There were guards stationed all round the walls, all dressed in flame colours and black tabards.

Each man carried a spear in his right hand, a short dagger at his side. Their faces were hidden by the visored helmets.

For the first time, Darius realized how threatening they looked, how difficult it was to regard them as ordinary men when you couldn't see their eyes. You knew they were watching you, but you could tell nothing from them. Darius knew that this was merely a trick to augment authority, but he found it disconcerting.

It was unbearably hot, standing to attention in that baking room. Darius could feel the sweat running down his back, pricking on his forehead. After a while the double doors at the far end of the chamber opened.

The guards round the wall all saluted. So did Darius and the others.

The Pyromancer entered the room. Darius assumed it was the same man who had run the tests the previous day, but there was no way of telling. The bronze helmet revealed nothing.

He said nothing, sweeping over the marble floor towards the conscripts, the cloth-of-gold cloak rustling against the stone floor.

They stood rigidly to attention while he looked them up and down, coming so close that Darius found it difficult to prevent himself flinching at the sickly stink of the Pyromancer's breath.

Having finished his inspection, the Pyromancer

moved back towards the brazier. They heard the soft crackle of flames as he stirred up the coals of fire.

"Your hands, gentlemen," he said quietly.

The guards round the wall moved suddenly forward, standing behind each of the new conscripts. Darius felt pressure beneath his left elbow. He found himself raising his hand, palm upwards, and saw that Perrian and the others had done the same.

The double door at the end of the hall opened once more.

A tall man in scarlet robes, his dark hair almost concealed by an open-faced version of the sunburst helmet, came striding along the hall towards them.

Beside them, the Pyromancer inclined his head in acknowledgement. Darius wondered whether he should salute or bow or something. This had to be Marrin, Earl of Bricus. But the others hadn't moved, and the soldier behind him gave no clue.

"You have done well," said Marrin. The words were warm but the Earl's voice was dry and parched as dust. "You have shown yourselves more able, physically and mentally, than your contemporaries. There is, however, one final test."

His black eyes gazed at them each in turn.

It was a long, considering gaze, one which seemed to search through Darius's character. And although there was a faint smile on Marrin's handsome face, Darius suddenly felt breathless. He did not trust this man, although there were lines of humour round his eyes, a mobile quality to the set of his mouth. Darius thought, this is a man who used to laugh. He doesn't now. Marrin was a strong man, from his build: wide shoulders, a thick-set neck, heavy hands. But he carried himself well, with dignity and surprising grace.

Without meaning to, with no consideration or forethought, Darius knew that he could like Marrin of Bricus. He wondered what would make this man laugh or cry or say anything direct and honest.

"I have something to ask of you. You may find this rather sudden, an intrusion in fact, but I have need of men like yourselves. Men I can trust." Marrin paused, calmly surveying them. "You have shown yourselves accomplished in all the skills of the warrior/courtier. With training, you might become part of the elite, of my own personal Guard.

"I ask of you one thing only. As a symbol of our trust in each other, as a proof of loyalty, I ask you to bear my insignia.

"I ask you to match your palms with mine."

He held up his left hand towards them and Darius saw that a sign had been branded on the palm, the sign of a dragon. It stood out on the flesh in a raised series of lumps.

For a moment the world shifted. Darius kept staring forward, as he had been trained to, but his mouth had gone quite dry, and his knees felt like jelly. He realized what the hissing sound to his left was.

An iron brand, glowing white hot in the heat of a brazier.

The Pyromancer was talking to them now. With difficulty, Darius dragged his eyes away from the other man's face.

"You have come this far, through ordeals of courage and skill and intelligence. All you have to prove now is that your heart is true, that you are willing to give your first loyalty to your lord and master here in Bricus. I ask each of you to accept the kiss of fire." He paused. "The rewards will be beyond imagining."

A silence then, one that went on for far too long. All Darius could think of was the hissing of that iron brand in the flames, how it would scorch against his flesh, the terrible pain of it.

He thought he might faint. And strangely that appalled him more than the prospect of pain. The shame of it, of passing out like some feeble girl in front of his friends! And when Jethro, one of the boys to his left, a nervy, complicated lad, suddenly broke rank, making for the door with stumbling, panicky steps, Darius could not stop himself from looking round. He saw Jethro fling himself against the door and one of the guards stepped forward. He made one short stab with his dagger, only one, and Jethro abruptly crumpled.

There was a horrible, moist thumping sound as Jethro's body collapsed to the floor. And all at once it became clear to Darius that there was no choice involved in this. He was not free to refuse the dragon brand.

He saw the Earl looking at him. His eyes were hooded.

"I have no use for men who run," Marrin said softly. "You can walk out of here, with all honour and dignity, and I promise that you will come to no harm. You can return to the ranks, and live the life of a soldier just like all the others. Or you can stay here, and become part of something else, something you will never regret. I promise you that. But there is one thing I must make clear. That I shall require loyalty unto death from you. And in return, you may require the same from me."

The Earl nodded to the Pyromancer.

"Now," he said to the white-faced conscripts. "Your hand on it?"

The burn took over a week to heal, but Darius hardly noticed it. They were given ointment to smear on the blisters, a crimson grease that reminded Darius of the smell he always associated with the Pyromancer. He wondered whether the peppery spice in all their food was part of the same magic, and was grateful for the anaesthetic power of the ointment.

Fire magic, he supposed. Strange, that he should find himself working alongside pyromancers when his family background was so very different! But he rarely thought of his family these days. For if the time in the conscript's camp had been hard, it was nothing to what happened to him now.

Exercises, drills, races, contests. They started before dawn, and finished only when it was no longer light enough to see a hand in front of the face. Their main meal took place at midday, mounds of roast meat and rice, with dishes of spicy vegetables. Then it was back on the athletics field again.

After dark they showered, and took a light supper before starting something else. Mental work this time. They were required to read vast tomes of military history and to recite dates of engagements and battles. They had to know the terms of every treaty that Bricus had signed, they had to realize which nations were enemies, which friendly, which neutral. They had to learn how each ship of the line was to be recognized, what their gunpower was, the number of their men and how they were rigged. This applied to the navies of neighbouring countries as well.

Then there were the rules of warfare, the

etiquette governing engagements. It was endless. But most difficult of all were the arbitrary and often meaningless regulations concerning behaviour at court. You could do the third button on your shirt up only if you had been in service for three years. You could part your hair on the left side only when wearing full dress uniform. A ring on the little finger betokened a position of ambassadorial rank. Time and again Darius found himself falling asleep over these dry texts, his head nodding between the pages.

It was Perrian who saved him from discovery. He seemed tireless, thirsty for knowledge and experience. Too often he woke Darius up with a sharp nudge in the ribs, even when there was no one there.

In the quad just before lights out, Darius grumbled at him. "You needn't have woken me this evening. The tutor wasn't even looking."

"But you were falling behind. You hadn't learned that last chapter and I knew you wouldn't want to be downgraded."

"Come on, Perrian, I wouldn't mind going back to the ranks, would you? Where's the fun in this?"

"Fun? Are you a child? This is about honour, Darius. You've been chosen, picked by the Earl himself to become part of his private Guard. What could possibly replace such glory?"

"I don't see much glory about this." Darius

scowled at Perrian. "We have to work like dogs all day long and then go back to school every night. Don't we get any time off?"

"I thought you were strong. A man waiting to be tempered like steel, someone who wanted to reach his ultimate potential. I thought you were a soldier, Darius, like your father. And if you're not stretched, how will you ever know what you are capable of?"

"Is that what *your* father tells you?" Sourly.

"Yes. He does." For a moment Perrian's eyes slid away from Darius.

"Well, where is your father?" Darius asked. "Why do we never see him?"

There was no answer. Perrian walked away towards the dormitory block as if he hadn't even heard Darius's question.

They were put through their paces by members of the Earl's Guard. They shared their meals with the senior members of the Guard, and pretty soon got to know them all by name, although informality was not encouraged. The Earl himself sometimes took them for archery practice, sessions which Darius particularly enjoyed.

He was almost unique in this. The other boys were greatly in awe of Marrin. They had grown up in Bricus, they had known the Earl's reputation all their lives. It was almost embarrassing to watch the way they flushed whenever he spoke to them.

Darius shared some of this awe, but he was confident in his abilities as an archer. He had always been good at this and his father had taken pains to give him plenty of practice back home. He was aware that the Earl watched him closely, and did his best to remember the things he had been taught.

He still didn't know who Perrian's father was. He couldn't remember seeing Perrian talking to any of the Guard or anyone paying special attention to him. He thought Perrian's father must have been on duty in another part of the palace.

"He's over there. The one they call Jasper," said Perrian, nodding to the far corner of the hallway, where a group of senior guards were smoking Sessera. The heavy scent wafted over the mosaic tiles towards them.

Jasper was a tall man, taller than the others, with glossy, gleaming hair caught back in a knot. He was burned brown as ebony by the sun, his skin a pattern of fine lines. He never once looked towards Perrian. He was laughing, his head thrown back, a full-throated roar. It was clear that the others followed his lead, chiming in with their own laughter once they'd heard Jasper.

"Why doesn't he ever talk to you?" Darius asked.

"Why should he? It would be like showing favouritism, it wouldn't be fair. I'd hate that and so would he."

"But – your father! Surely you can say hello to each other?" It didn't make sense to Darius.

"If you're so keen on family relationships, why did you run away from home?"

"It wasn't running away. We came for the festival."

"Well, that was a waste of time, wasn't it?" Perrian laughed contemptuously.

Darius ignored him. "It's my sister I worry about," he said.

"A *girl*! If she's stupid enough to leave her parents' protection, she can't be worth anything much—"

Darius had had enough. Although he was tired out from the day's exertions, he surged to his feet, swinging wildly with his right fist.

Perrian was caught off balance. It would never have worked otherwise. He fell sideways to the ground, his head knocking against the bench with a sharp crack.

He lay there unmoving, white-faced.

A crowd gathered, and a lieutenant began issuing instructions. Someone went to bring water, someone else ran for the apothecary. There was a certain amount of fuss, but scraps were not uncommon among the conscripts. During all the explanations and reprimands, Darius kept wondering where Jasper was.

Wouldn't he be concerned about his son?

Wouldn't he even come to ask what had happened? But Jasper stayed over the other side of the quad. He didn't even look to see what all the fuss was about. He moved with a group of friends towards the refectory and didn't look round.

Darius watched him go.

CHAPTER 9

Dreaming

There were three levels of command within the Earl's personal Guard. There were the Seniors, the men who were the Earl's closest confidants, including Jasper and his friends; the Mediators, from whom most of the instructors were drawn; and the Initiates, just a year or so above Darius's own level.

Their ages ranged between fourteen and thirtyish. And Darius, increasingly admired for his archery skills and determined effort, was beginning to make friends with them all.

The Pyromancer had his own hierarchy of acolytes and servants. As far as Darius could work out, those higher up the ladder wore the more elaborate, concealing helmets. These strange men with their hidden faces and long robes never mixed with the Guard. Sometimes Darius passed one of them in a corridor and the spicy, sickly scent from the man's clothes lingered with him for some time.

Perrian was not seriously injured. He appeared at training on the following day, looking a little pale but otherwise all right. They were in the armoury, picking out swords for the next practice session.

As Darius buckled on one of the short broadswords the Earl's Guard favoured, Perrian came up to him. "I believe I offended you yesterday. I'm sorry. I should not have criticized members of your family."

Darius glanced at him. "It doesn't matter. I'm glad you're better..."

There were severe straight lines drawn between his brows. Darius wondered idly if Perrian ever laughed. He felt rather sorry for him. "It's OK," he said. "Forget it."

Perrian gave a small smile and held out his hand. Darius took it. He thought that probably he could consider Perrian a friend. He rather liked the idea; he'd not had a male friend before.

He'd always had Laura. With a shock, he realized how little he'd thought of her recently. He'd made no effort to find out what had happened to her. He couldn't understand how he could have forgotten her. Had he gone mad? What had happened?

He'd been run off his feet of course. The answer slotted easily into his mind. Every night he fell into a dreamless sleep and there was no time for quiet reflection... It was as if this exclusively male society had made Laura's existence irrelevant. There were no women anywhere within the palace. Even the cooks and cleaners were men.

From afar, Darius watched the ordinary soldiers, the conscripts who had failed the tests, undergoing their exercises and drills on the far side of the quad. It seemed to him that they were more free, more lighthearted. Certainly they were closer to the world of the city.

"Do the ranks ever get out into the city?" he asked one of the Mediators one day.

"Only if they've proved themselves. We allow trusties to visit their families, if they want to." The man looked speculatively at Darius. "Why, do you want to get out?"

Darius paused before replying. The memory of Jethro's body tumbling to the ground made him hesitate. What would be considered disloyal, what would be seen as weakness?

"I didn't have a chance to tell anyone where I am," he said carefully. "My family won't know what happened. They'll be worrying."

"Too bad." The man laughed. "If they've been

sheltering you from the draft, they deserve all they've got coming." And then he said, more kindly, "You can send a note, I suppose. I'll get one of the boys round to take it to your family."

"Thanks. I'd really appreciate that." It was a start, he thought. He could get them to try at the Silver Street address … someone might know.

"Well, you're a promising soldier. It's been noticed, you know, the way you handle a bow." The man's hand on his arm was friendly and re-assuring. "A small tip, from an old soldier – don't think too much about home. That's all behind you now. Look forward to your life here in the palace, it has its consolations. There's honour to be found here, in the service of the Earl. You'll see."

Darius watched him go. The Mediator held himself upright, striding across the quad as if he owned it.

"Where's all this honour then?" said Darius to Perrian that evening. "What's it all in aid of? Are we at war? What's the great cause?"

"You really do know nothing, don't you?" It wasn't really a put-down. "It's the aquemancers. They've been banned from Bricus and we have to make sure that the city is kept free of water-magic."

"How do we do that?"

"Why do you think we sweat our guts out with all this training, Darius? We have to be on our toes,

95

mentally and physically, to hunt out water-witches. They're underhand, subversive, treacherous. No one knows quite what's happened to them all. They're lying low somewhere, that's for sure, and probably planning some kind of rebellion."

"What's so wrong with them? What have they done?"

"They've enchanted the Countess. Led her astray, so that she betrayed the Earl's trust. They're power mad, wanting to oust the Earl –"

"Really?" Dimly, Darius remembered what he knew of aquemancers. Wincy, for example. Subtle, clever, sharp… Treachery might well be part of the deal. "But what can we do against magic?" Darius asked.

"We have to be ready for it," said Perrian. "A healthy mind in a healthy body. It's our only chance. We have to find the water-witches, and then turn them over to the Pyromancer. He can handle aquemancers, don't you worry."

Darius felt himself alert with curiosity.

That evening there was a knock at the library door. Someone called out, "Darius! It's for you."

He put down the heavy book he was struggling with and went to the door. Franklin was there, standing smartly to attention. "At your service, sir," he said, looking straight ahead. "I was told you had a message."

For a moment Darius couldn't remember what he meant. And then it hit him. Laura. How could he have forgotten? What was happening to him?

"Yes, that's right." Darius slipped out, closing the door behind him. "Lord, Franklin, how did you swing a messenger's job?"

"I'm no good for anything else." But there was a crinkling at the side of his eyes and Darius felt more cheerful.

"Can you really find someone for me in Bricus?" he asked, much relieved.

"If you've a name and address, yes, of course. Who is it?"

"My sister." Darius told Franklin her name. "The trouble is I've no idea where she'll be. I haven't seen or heard of her since I was pressed."

"And she's a stranger here?" Franklin looked doubtful. "It'll be difficult," he said. "Unless she's been very lucky the slavers or thief masters will have got her. But I'll try. What was that address you were making for?"

Darius gave him Wincy's address in Silver Street. Then he scribbled a brief note and folded it with Laura's name on the outside. "Let me know," he said. "It's important."

"You're twins, aren't you?" Franklin looked thoughtful. "I'll do my best, don't worry."

He saluted again and marched away through the olive groves to the barracks.

Darius returned to the library almost unaware of the way his fists were clenching.

He would never forgive himself if anything had happened to Laura. His parents would never forgive him, he'd never be able to go home. He would have to stay here, amongst all these strangers, forever cut off, forever alone... Why did he keep forgetting Laura? His memory was usually reliable, but here he went for hours, days without thinking of her. He didn't understand what was happening and for a moment he seriously considered making a break for it, trying to escape somehow.

But then Perrian beckoned him over and asked him something about strategy and together they studied a map of the Garnet mountains where one of the Ledlan warlords was expanding their territory, getting dangerously near the northern boundaries of Bricus...

Again, it was all too easy to forget about Laura.

"From this moment on, you are never alone." The Pyromancer stared at them through the wafting smoke. "You are now part of a brotherhood which will endure to death and beyond. You are bonded by more than ties of family and blood. This is the life you have chosen, one earned through the sweat of your body, the concentration of your mind. You wear the mark of the dragon on your hand. Be proud of it. You may trust with your life any man who wears the same mark. You will never be alone again, and courage and faith will sustain you for ever."

They were standing to attention in front of a steaming cauldron of flaming sandalwood.

The Pyromancer was facing them, his hands held wide, concealed by their heavy gauntlets. He said, "You are here to become pure, cleansed of past sins, of evil influences, of your past lives. You will be born afresh this day, into the most glorious company of all. You are ready. Now, empty your mind of daily cares and worries. Receive the breath of sanctity."

He leaned forward slightly and blew into the smoke.

Immediately Darius's eyes began to water. He found the breath choking in his throat. He was beginning to gasp.

And then it struck. Like a shaft of white light it cut through his thoughts, releasing him. He felt separated: suspended, god-like, far above his own body.

With some interest he observed the blank and fishy expression on his own face. But this face, with its familiar planes and creases was mundane and boring, totally without animation. He looked away, drawn by the flaming mask of the Pyromancer.

He was lifting his hands, lifting away the mask

and Darius suddenly wanted to stop it all, to get back inside his poor, stupid-looking body and not see whatever lay behind the mask.

The helmet lifted and the sight shrieked through Darius's mind. A dragon's head. A man with the long, equine head of a dragon, smoke billowing from the nostrils, mad red eyes glowing blood-red and frighteningly intelligent.

It wriggled its body and the cloth-of-gold cloak fell away.

Beneath it were wings and a scaled, elongated body. This was neither man nor ordinary dragon. This was something quite different.

A firefly, made of flesh.

And it spoke to them, although it had no mouth and made no sound. Its words slid into Darius's mind, sibilant as rustling leaves.

"It thrills, it lives and entices, the kiss of fire..."

And it really felt like that. There was a buzz of excitement running through his thoughts, as if someone had lit sparklers in his mind.

He was aware that they were all with him, Perrian and the Earl and Jasper and all the other Seniors and Mediators and Initiates, and that the other acolytes were there too, darting among the new recruits, and there was a kind of wild dance going on, something that involved them all, drawing him in, burning away the memories of the past.

CHAPTER 10

Aquemancy

That evening, in a backstreet inn, in a booth tucked away near the kitchens, Quinland explained to Laura about water-witches. Aquemancy took many forms, he said. In other lands it was rumoured that water-witches could tell the future by looking into pools of water. But here in Bricus different skills had developed. The most powerful and useful of these skills was the ability to influence the weather, but only a very few aquemancers could achieve that. In fact, he only knew two: the Countess Philomena and her lady-in-waiting, his beloved Wincy Alderwood.

"She's extraordinary," he said, shaking his head. "It's in her eyes or her hands or a bit of both, I can never quite decide. But magic runs through her, influences her every thought, rules everything about her. During the emergency, when we first realized what Lerris was up to, it was Wincy who discovered the use of the watery transformation, the way aquemancers can, as a last resort, protect themselves –"

"By disappearing into a different dimension?"

"The dreaming dimension … yes. And leaving a little water behind as a link, of course. I can see that Max has been explaining." He frowned. "I hope he has also impressed upon you the need for secrecy." In the flickering candlelight, he looked increasingly serious. "If only it had not been so rushed! Only a few weeks more and Wincy would have been able to share her knowledge. As it was, she only had time to show me and the Countess how to release them," he said. "I've been teaching Randall, and he knows more or less what to do. It's a long-winded method, of course. There's no one else, as far as I know."

"Do you know which bottles are the right ones in advance?" asked Laura.

"If only we did… No. We have to open each bottle carefully, one by one, following a certain, rather fiddly and precise ritual. Nine times out of ten – no, more than that – ninety-five per cent of the time there's nothing there. And of that remaining five per cent, half might be nightmares, something dragged through from the dreaming dimension by aquemancers to confuse others. Perhaps one in a thousand is a real aquemancer..."

"Was that a nightmare I released today?" Laura asked. She was clasping her hands together rather hard.

"Sounds like it. But don't worry about what you did." He put his hand on her shoulder and frowned. "Unless the Pyromancer has been at work. He may even be using the dreaming himself. This would be the worst kind of bad luck, but it's not your fault at all."

She wanted to believe him so much. "Perhaps you should teach me what to look for," she said slowly, remembering Max's fury that they hadn't told her the significance of the bottles. "I think you should tell me everything. So I can help, next time." She kept her eyes on Randall as she said this, daring him to interrupt.

Randall put down his pint mug and minutely shook his head at Quinland. He looked very doubtful but Quinland took no notice. He was studying Laura as if he'd never seen her before. Then he leaned forward and took hold of her left hand, turning it over as if he were going to read her palm. Gently his fingers traced the slight remnants of webbing between her little and ring fingers.

He made no comment but his eyes widened. There was a pause before he said, "Very well. I don't see why not." He stood up from the table, taking his jacket from the back of the chair.

"Where are you going?" asked Randall in surprise.

"There's no time like the present. Come on, Randall. We could do with an apprentice."

"Max. Or Nina. They're half-way there already and we don't have the time to teach someone else –"

"I don't get this, Randall!" Laura was on her feet too, her voice raised. "Why do I have to be excluded all the time? All right, so it wasn't very clever to arrive here without telling anyone. But I'm not usually stupid, you know that, and you must have been fifteen once too –"

"It's not that I think you're stupid. Far from it. But the more you know, the more dangerous it could be for you."

"How? How can *knowing* make things worse?" It was desperately important to her that she should make no further mistakes.

"Randall actually means that your knowing will make things more dangerous for all of us," said Quinland plainly. Randall looked furiously at him.

"But I'd never give you away!" Laura cried.

"You might not be able to help yourself," said Randall. "I don't want you hurt."

She believed him, looking at those fine, serious eyes. He had her best interests at heart, all along.

He had always looked out for her, just like Darius. But...

"But if you need help, an extra pair of hands, at least you know you can trust me."

"True enough." He smiled ruefully and ruffled her hair as if she was a child again. He stood up, pulling up the hood of his cloak to cover his bright hair. "Shall we gather up Max and Nina on the way?" he said to Quinland. "They could do with a bit of practice."

"They're probably there already," said Quinland.

Together the three of them left the inn and went out into the night streets.

In the early evening the streets were still crowded. They pushed their way through the hot, sweaty masses and Laura gradually realized that there was another smell about the place. The air was slightly cloudy with smoke and then she saw that there were flaming torches attached to every wall. The fountains and statuary in the city squares had sheaves of burning twigs draped all over them. Clouds of spicy scented smoke drifted everywhere, and people were coughing and spluttering, complaining loudly.

There were helmeted soldiers standing at every corner, every junction, guarding the burning torches. They were surveying the crowds, although it was difficult to tell for sure. Laura could see nothing behind the bronze visors every man wore. It made her even more uneasy.

"Why have we got to breathe in this stuff?" she whispered to Randall, catching his sleeve.

He was about to reply and then he indicated a small skirmish a few metres away across the market place from where they were standing.

One of the soldiers had a street urchin by the shoulder, and was holding him still while another soldier frisked him.

They found nothing: a quick cuff to the boy's head and then they let him go, turning back to confer about something.

Laura was going to say something but Randall's grip on her arm tightened. She stood very still, watching as the urchin rubbed his sleeve over his face and plumped down on a doorstep behind one of the stalls.

She almost missed it, the way his other hand sneaked down the side of the step, the glint of something shiny caught in the bright torchlight. A bottle, hastily slipped beneath the boy's shirt. He looked up then, and flashed a grin towards Randall and Quinland.

"That's Shimmy," said Randall to Laura as they made their way on through the square. "One of us."

"How many are you?" she asked breathlessly.

She was having to run every few steps to keep up with Randall and Quinland.

"Not enough," he answered. "Not by half. And fewer all the time…" He looked so tired that she wondered if he was ill. "This way," he said shortly, pulling her to one side.

They were passing along the wall of a tall town house. Laura had noticed no door but a tangled overspilling of dying vines and clematis hung down from a second-floor balcony. Quinland had already slipped behind the curtain of greenery and Randall held the foliage away from the wall so that Laura could see the door behind.

She followed Quinland into a crystal world of colour and light.

It was a hallway lined with shelves. Each shelf was crowded with hundreds of bottles. They were crammed so closely together that their rims over-hung the edge.

Overhead a chandelier burned brightly. She heard voices a long way off and the occasional chink of glass. It sounded like a party except that there was no laughter. No music.

The hallway reached the length of the house. A sweeping staircase led up to the higher floors and there were bottles crammed to the sides of each step too, leaving only a narrow passage in the centre.

Doors opened on to rooms full of heavy antique

furniture. There were dressers and sideboards and tables and whatnots, and every single surface was covered with glassware. "There must be thousands of bottles here!" she said, aghast.

"Yes. And we have to test each and every one of them."

She understood his tiredness, his short temper now. "You come here every night?" she said.

He nodded. "Quin says short cat naps are enough to keep going, but I'm not entirely convinced."

She watched the retreating figure of Quinland far ahead of them. Every now and then he picked a bottle from one of the shelves and placed it carefully in his string bag. "What's he doing now?" she asked, puzzled.

"Sometimes you get a hunch – a feeling – that one bottle is more likely than the others. Quin's better at it than I, but it's still a low success rate."

"Could I try? What do you look for?"

Randall shrugged. "It's difficult to describe. It would be easy if we knew... There's nothing specific, you see. You have to trust to intuition."

As they walked she looked at the thousands of bottles, green, gold, brown, blue, clear. They reminded her of the arrangement of bottles on the shelf in her bedroom back home, except there were so many here. There was no real comparison. Every now and then she followed Quinland and Randall's example and took one down. By the time they had reached the back kitchen to the rear of the house, her arms were full.

Max and Nina were already there, unpacking and arranging bottles on shelves. The room was dominated by the vast, ancient, iron range, mercifully unlit. There was little other furniture: a few chairs, a table, covered with crockery and the remains of food. Every other surface, every bench, sideboard, window-sill and rack, was covered with bottles. Even the china sink under the shuttered window was full of them.

Quinland threw off his jacket and rolled up his sleeves. He sat down on a small stool by the range and took a magnifying glass from his trouser pocket. With it he examined in minute detail a small green bottle, tilting it this way and that in the light from the oven. Then he lit the wick of a gas-lamp standing on the table and in that much brighter, clearer light, examined the bottle once more.

He nodded to himself, and put the magnifying glass down. Carefully he eased the stopper from the bottle and smelled the contents. His nose wrinkled: the bottle was hurled into a basket by the wall where it shattered amongst the remains of many others. Without pause, he took another up and repeated the process.

Randall had pulled up a stool opposite Quinland. He indicated that Laura should sit next to him. Max and Nina had already settled themselves on the other side of Randall.

He said, "First you have to look. This is the most important stage of all. In the clear light from the lamp and in firelight. A magnifying lens is useful, but not essential. Any cloudiness and disturbance, or dust or matter in the liquid and it's no good. Throw it. No aquemancer would risk using dirty liquid. Only then, when the most detailed visual examination has taken place, then, carefully, slowly, *gently*, take the stopper out." He demonstrated, twisting the neck of the bottle.

A sour, bitter smell. Vinegary wine, ancient and unmistakable.

A smash as the bottle hit the basket of shards. Randall picked up another one.

And another. And another. "Any smell at all and it's no use. Water-witches *only* use the purest water," said Randall.

Most failed at the first visual inspection. Some of the others were thrown out after opening. They all took turns in smelling white spirit, gin, salt, oranges, disinfectant, soap. There were worse things: organic waste, chemicals, foul-smelling concoctions that made them want to retch.

"Try this," said Laura, handing Randall one of the bottles she'd chosen because it looked like one of her collection at home. He took it from her, holding it up to the light, subjecting it to the same meticulous examination. A slight frown, as he gently unscrewed the stopper and sniffed the contents. A look of intense concentration on his face as he handed it to each of them in turn.

Laura could smell nothing. Max also shook his head. But Nina frowned and tried again.

"I'm not sure," she said at last. "A slight saltiness perhaps?" Randall took it back from her and tried again.

"I don't know…" He handed it to Quinland.

"Did you choose this one?" Quinland asked Laura. She nodded. "Right. Well, I think you deserve to try the next stage."

"But –" began Randall.

"Let her," said Quinland. "It's hers by right. Now," he said to Laura, "hold the bottle between finger and thumb of your left hand, like *that* –" He demonstrated.

She took the bottle from him, aware that her hands were very slightly shaky. He held out to her an eye-dropper. "Take only a small amount of liquid from the bottle, to check the colour," he said. "A drop or two, no more…"

She did as instructed. The water was glacier-clear. "Put the drops back now," he said softly, "and come with me." He led her to an open cupboard to the side of the room. It was rather cold, set well back from the range, a dark, long and narrow room. The butler's pantry, she suddenly realized, although it looked nothing like the one at home.

The walls and floor were lined with cushions, padded with the softest silks and velvets.

In the centre of the chamber, a small dish stood on the floor, on a swathe of green silk. Laura knew what to do: she looked at Quinland, who nodded.

Carefully she made her way through the silken puffs of colour to the dish. With hands that now shook painfully, she poured the contents of the bottle into the dish. She was aware that they were all watching her.

"Wait there," said Quinland, when the bottle was empty. "Now, I have to convince our water-witch, if we do have one here, that he or she can re-emerge in this place of safety. I have to catch his or her attention in the dreaming, and reveal the way home."

"How – ?" He put his finger across his lips. And then he sat down on one of the cushions at the far end of the alcove and held out his hands. Laura carefully placed the bowl in his upturned palms.

He closed his eyes. At once she moved back out of the chamber. It was very quiet; Nina and Max had fallen silent, and Randall was standing beside her, watching with close attention, some anxiety on his face.

Laura was staring at the bowl in Quinland's hands so intently that her eyes were watering. His hands were perfectly steady, and not a ripple disturbed the surface of the water. And then she realized that Quinland was murmuring something under his breath, the faintest sequence of words, a ceaseless incantation she did not recognize. In fact, she could hardly hear it at all.

Nothing seemed to happen for a very long time. Just the quiet murmuring, the stillness of concentration and the faint sounds of street life outside the kitchen window.

Was there a mist arising from the bowl? Laura couldn't really tell. But Quinland's features were blurred now, as if seen through contoured glass.

Randall's hand on her shoulder tightened. Quinland's voice seemed to be failing. She could hear nothing now, and no one moved.

She thought later that she must have fallen asleep. That, for a few brief seconds she had been unconscious, because when she looked again there was someone else there. Opposite Quinland, his eyes closed, a strange old man sat cross-legged on the pile of cushions. His gnarled old hands were peacefully folded on his lap and as she looked his eyes suddenly sprang open.

His thin lips smiled as he leaned forward and stretched out one hand to touch Quinland.

"Quin," he said, softly. "It's all right, my old friend, my *very* good old friend!"

Quinland's own eyes were open now, glinting

in the dim light. He put the bowl down and reached forward. For a moment the two men clasped hands.

"Welcome home, Ross! Welcome, indeed!" said Quinland, getting to his feet. He put out his hand again to help the old man up and the old man came stumbling to standing. He seemed very unsteady on his feet and Laura realized at last why the chamber was so padded, so soft with cushions. It was designed to receive people who had survived an extraordinary transformation...

"Ross!" Randall moved into the chamber. "Take it easy man, it takes a while –"

"I know, I know!" But the old man was almost laughing while all the time his eyes scanned his surroundings. "Still in hiding, are we? Things no better?"

Quinland shook his head. "There's a suspicion that the Pyromancer has access to the dreaming now. But we have a recruit here," he said, beckoning Laura forward. "This is Laura Brooke, who found your linking flask."

"My gratitude, sweet lady!" Although he was clearly weak and unsteady, he nonetheless managed a creditable bow. "Forgive my clumsiness!"

"I'm so glad I was able to help," she said shyly.

"Beginner's luck," said Randall. It sounded slightly sour.

"Perhaps," said Quinland. "Although Laura

shares your and Wincy's heritage, of course."

"What do you mean?" Randall looked suspicious. Quinland raised an eyebrow.

"Why, you and Wincy are both aquemancers. Laura is your cousin, an Alderwood by birth. Why should she not share the same talent? She has the remains of webbing on her hand. You know what *that* means."

"Her mother, my aunt Cytheria, has no such skill."

"You mean, you've never seen it. Many water-witches are reluctant to practise. It draws attention, and that can bring trouble."

"Nonsense. It's luck, whether you can do it or not."

Laura listened to this with amazement. It came to her that Randall was jealous of his skill and didn't want to acknowledge that his young cousin might share it.

The old aquemancer quickly revived. He and Quinland conferred together for a while and then he left, sketching another elaborate bow towards Laura.

Quinland and Randall returned to their work. Systematically they examined bottle after bottle, and very few survived even that first visual inspection. But even that took a minute or so.

There were tens of thousands of bottles in the house and more were being collected every day. It was an endless task. Max and Nina were constantly busy, bringing likely specimens to Randall or Quinland's attention. For a while Laura helped them and then she remembered the armful of bottles she had collected on the way through the hallway.

They were still together, neatly arranged on the floor by the door to the hall. Carefully, she took one up and passed it to Quinland.

And it worked. The close examination, the use of the dropper, the movement of them all over to the chamber. Laura was so keyed up that when Quinland began his quiet chanting, she almost jumped.

She missed it again, the moment of manifestation. One moment Quinland was there all on his own, his eyes closed, his hands holding the bowl and the next there was someone sitting opposite him on the cushions.

This time the stranger was a young girl. "Oh, Lally, my dear!" Quinland was on his feet immediately, picking her up off the cushions and clasping her to his chest. He was smiling, thrilled to have found someone who was clearly very special to him.

And yet, watching, Laura saw that Randall was frowning, hanging back. And then she realized the answer to it, why he was being so difficult. He'd been hoping for Wincy, of course, that was it. And then he stepped forward and embraced the girl and introduced her to Laura and in the excitement, Laura forgot that the only two successes that night had been found in bottles she had chosen.

After Lally's release, Quinland asked Randall to take Lally home. "And this young lady looks tired," he continued, twinkling at Laura. "Perhaps you should take her back to Silver Street, too."

"We've hardly started."

"But we've done really well, don't you think? And you can always come back afterwards, can't you?" said Quinland reasonably. "We'll need to get on."

They left Lally with her mother, a pale, worn-looking, middle-aged woman working late in a small shack near the river. She was a seamstress, but at first Laura couldn't work out where her customers would come from. Lally's mother, whose name was Marguerite, explained that she was in hiding here. The Pyromancer had searched the area quite recently, and Marguerite felt that they would be safe there, for a time at least.

This was a poor area. The stink from the rotting waste piled up at the sides of the narrow channel of water was overwhelming. The huts and shacks clinging to the river bank all looked temporary, haphazardly flung together out of old gates and doors, of sheets of corrugated iron and packing cases.

Marguerite was ecstatic to have her daughter restored. Their joy was infectious, but Randall and Laura didn't stay long. Randall was in a hurry to get back to Quinland and their endless task.

"Will you be all right on your own here?" he said, having settled Laura back in the room beneath the garden shed.

"Randall – try the bottles I put down on the floor by the door. Give them a go."

"Are they the ones you chose?"

She nodded. "Lally and Ross both came from bottles I'd picked."

"Really, my dear?" He smiled at her, but it only made her feel uncomfortable. "Well, I shall certainly try them first of all." He chucked her under the chin, as if she was a baby, and disappeared through the trapdoor without further delay.

She wasn't tired. She wasn't remotely sleepy. She fidgeted around the room for a bit, even lay down for a while, but she couldn't settle.

In a way she was too excited. She had no doubt that she'd picked the relevant bottles that night. She knew that the others on that small table were also likely to be special. She wondered whether she too shared Wincy and Randall's magic skill. Why, with training, perhaps she'd be able to make rainbows and fountains and rivers to flow… And she remembered how her mother had always been so certain of the weather…

"No, it's going to rain today," she'd say, on bright clear mornings when Darius and Laura wanted to wear sandals to school. She always knew when to plant out seeds, when to bring the washing in.

It was part of water magic, to predict the weather. Laura had never noticed it happen but Darius had grumbled. "How does she *know*?" he complained, changing his clothes yet again. "Why is she always *right*?"

Remembering Darius was like a physical blow to her. She hadn't remembered him, not for one moment, throughout that entire day.

And at last she knew why she couldn't settle. She had never been away from him for so long before. She wanted to tell him about Randall and Quinland and Max and Nina and Ross and Lally. She couldn't bear that she should be knowing and experiencing so much and that he should be out of it all.

There was nothing she could do. She lay down on the pile of blankets which served as a bed and waited for Randall's return, her eyes open against the dark.

CHAPTER 11

Wincy

arius was asleep, the deep stupor of physical and mental exhaustion. The dormitory he shared with Perrian and the others was disturbed only by sounds of breathing and the odd snore. Moonlight, creeping through the crossbars on the window, spread velvet shadows on the floor.

He dreamed of water.

It was unsurprising, given the nature of the day's activities. Long-distance running had been the main event, followed by two hours' drill out in the roasting quad. They'd been slacking, the Senior said. They had to perform the same manoeuvres again and again. Darius had been ragingly thirsty all the time.

So he dreamed of water, dripping. Like rain through a hole in the roof, he dreamed of the irregular falling of single drops. It was irritating in a way. What he wanted was a gush of coolness over his head, down his throat. But this sequence of drops pricked into his sleep, making him toss and turn until his sheets were all bundled up into a tight ball.

And for a while he was disorientated, lying there in the dormitory, because something was out of place, something was wrong.

There was water falling from the ceiling, falling into a puddle by his bedside. He sat up, staring at it.

There was no drumming of rain on the roof, no lines of water running down the window. Yet water was dripping from the wooden joist over his head and he couldn't understand where it was coming from.

He stood on his bed, reaching up to the joist and pulling himself up to look over the top of it. Nothing. It was perfectly dry. He sat down on the bed again, more than a little puzzled.

The puddle on the floor was growing. Rather, it was changing shape, elongating itself until it spread over several floorboards at once. As he watched, fascinated, it began to run across the floor towards the door, flowing smoothly over the rough wood.

He leaned forwards to watch it and a drop of icy water fell on the back of his neck. It tingled there, needling him into movement. He was irritated now, quite angry at being disturbed. He was going to find out what was going on. This was all ridiculous.

So he pulled on his breeches and boots and a shirt, and took his knife belt and before he knew it he was at the door to the dormitory, fully dressed and ready for action.

The moving puddle of water flowed beneath it.

He put out his hand to push the door and it swung open, lightly and easily. Someone must have forgotten to lock it, he told himself. Or the catch was faulty. But one part of him knew that this could not be so. Something else had opened that door, had drawn him from the bed and made him get dressed and was luring him away from the dormitory, reeling him in like a fish on a line.

The pool of water was moving quite swiftly now, flowing down each step in a series of mini-waterfalls. He had to quicken his step to keep up with it and when it reached the bottom he was not at all surprised to find that the double doors were not only unlocked (something unknown in his experience) but also swinging silently open before his approach.

He did not think the word "magic" to himself,

but every instinct knew that this was something extraordinary, something which he, one of the Earl's chosen Guard, should shun. He should report this, wake up his colleagues, go and get one of the Seniors.

He did nothing of the sort. An unusual lethargy stopped him. He was curious, he told himself, that was what it was. He should find out what was going on and investigate. (*But you also come from a family of aquemancers*, said a voice within him. *Water is significant to you…*) He followed the moving pool of water, treading carefully and quietly, and it was as if the scar on his hand meant nothing at all.

It led him through silent corridors and down empty staircases. He crossed hallways paved with iridescent marble, where lion shapes and phoenixes briefly came to life beneath the moving contour of water.

The palace's west gate was ajar. The light in the gatekeeper's office was on and through the window Darius saw the man sitting at his desk, his head leaning on his hand. His eyes were closed and he was snoring.

With no hesitation at all Darius slipped through the gate. It swung shut behind him and he looked round, worried that any slight noise might wake the gatekeeper. There was no sound, but even then he didn't begin to suspect that he might be

123

dreaming. There was nothing, no movement or hasty shout.

He turned round and found himself face to face with Wincy.

She hugged him, just as she always used to and there was something so cool and fresh about her, something familiar that reminded him of home so sharply that he felt a lump in his throat.

She had changed. Her eyes seemed darker than before, more serious. Her hair was touched with grey and she somehow seemed a little indistinct round the edges, not quite as definite, as dominating as he remembered. All these things worried him. But she turned aside his questions and asked him instead what he was doing in Bricus, in the Earl's palace.

So he found himself blurting out the whole story, all about coming to Bricus and losing Laura and joining the Earl's company.

"Oh, Darius, what have you got yourself into?" she said sadly, but he had the uneasy suspicion that she was surprised by none of it.

She had him by the arm, hurrying him along with her usual quick pace. They seemed to whisk through the city, their feet hardly touching the ground. Streets and shops and squares flashed by in a blur of grey and silver light.

He thought distractedly, am I dreaming?

Wincy was waiting for his answer.

"I was pressed," he repeated defensively, as the city whirled around him. "I didn't mean to get involved in all this."

Her sharp grey eyes glanced at him. They held him steady, for a moment. "You always wanted to be a soldier, didn't you? And I'd heard that the Earl's own Guard was handpicked."

He remembered how he'd always been soothed by her calm voice, her graceful, unobtrusive movements. And yet she was cleverer by far than he was, cleverer than anyone he knew.

"The Earl isn't a bad man," he protested, aware that these words were inadequate. He tried again. "It's a great honour to be in his company, and I've sworn loyalty to him..." He sounded very stiff, even to his own ears.

They were passing swiftly through well-to-do boulevards, out of reach of the palace or the militia. A faint breeze lifted through his hair, freshened on his cheek. He was hardly aware of moving: it was more as if the city was falling behind, dropping away.

Wincy moved smoothly, gracefully, her grey cloak flowing behind her in this same faint, light wind. She had not replied to his statement beyond another of those unsettling glances.

"And what has he told you to do? What do the Earl's men *do* with their time?"

"We train. Exercises, drill, that kind of thing."

"Do you know to what purpose?"

He was silent.

"Well, shall I tell you, dear Darius, what your principal duty will be?"

The movement had stilled. Wincy was standing blocking his way, her eyes blazing.

He wanted to shrink back, to get away. Suddenly, she looked very frightening.

There was nothing behind him. No sense of the city, no pattern of roads and squares. Only greyness, a drab emptiness.

"Where are we? Oh, Wincy, what's happening?"

She ignored his questions. Her voice struck out, shattering through his thoughts.

"You'll be required to hunt out aquemancers. You'll have to track them down as if they were vermin. You'll have to arrest anyone who looks remotely suspicious, and turn them over to the Pyromancer's Court. Then you'll have to supervise the executions, stand to attention and salute while women and men and children are burned to cinders by fireflies!"

She lifted her hand and for a moment he saw the greyness around them take the shape of flames, and writhing limbs. Hands held out, blackening, charring, mouths open, screaming.

"It's not like that!" he shouted. He was desperate, sickened by the vision, even as it faded back into the greyness. "We train and we study

126

history and military law and no one's said *anything* about aquemancy!" But he remembered Perrian, nonetheless.

"They will. Listen to me, Darius, you'll soon be out there with the rest of them, patrolling the streets, ruining people's lives—"

"Wincy! What are you talking about?" He couldn't stand the way she was going on, he couldn't bear what she was saying, what she was showing him.

She was pulling away from him, retreating into the grey nothingness. It was everywhere now, blotting out the city, blotting out anything he recognized. He was frantic. Was she going to leave him here, lost in this dreadful place? He was truly frightened by her behaviour and her words, but worst of all was where he was.

He didn't understand it, didn't know what was happening. Was he asleep? He hoped, more than anything, that this was merely a dream.

He put his hand out, trying to touch something, anything, but there was nothing. He could hear nothing, see nothing. All his senses were muffled by the greyness. How could she abandon him here?

"Wincy!" he cried. "Wincy, where are you?"

The sound was swallowed up. He could not tell if it had carried at all.

But there she was again, coming into focus

before him like a reflection in a stilling puddle. She faced him again. "Perhaps you'd better return to the palace," she said and he could hear only sadness in her voice. "You'll find out sooner or later the truth of what I say."

"I believe you! Wincy, I just didn't understand! Of course I know you're telling the truth!"

Wincy was his cousin, someone he'd always trusted, always relied on and respected. She'd not let him down, any more than his mother would.

She studied his face in the grey wastelands of the dreaming and he wondered what she saw there. He thought again, with a chill, that she had changed. There was something slippery, indistinct about her. She had withdrawn from him.

"Very well." That unnerving gaze, demanding too much from him. "I'm risking everything now, Darius. I'm taking a chance because we have no choice, but if you betray us, if you let me down, I –" She stopped.

"I won't! Of course I won't betray you, how could I?"

"Even with this?" She gestured to the embroidered dragon on the front of his tabard.

"You're family, Wincy! How could you think it? I'd as soon betray Laura!" What was he saying? Hadn't he already betrayed his sister? He hadn't even thought of her for days!

"Listen well, Darius. This is crucial. This is

about your life and mine. I'm going to take you to meet someone very important, someone whose identity and whereabouts you *must* keep secret. It's a question of life and death," she repeated. "I'm trusting you here, Darry."

His childhood nickname disarmed him. He nodded numbly.

She passed her hand over his eyes and there was a moment of pain, something confusing and disorientating, as if he'd suddenly got soap in his eyes. He rubbed them and when he looked again everything had changed.

The dreadful greyness had gone: instead, he found himself in a forest.

It was all around him. Widely spaced trees formed avenues of green light, their branches dipping towards him. Leaves waved softly over his face, gentle as water.

For the first time for weeks he felt cool. There was grass beneath his feet, waving round his ankles. He reached his hand towards the leaves and dew or rain refreshed his skin.

The strange spicy fog in which he had lived at the palace had lifted. He saw things with brighter, clearer, colours. Emerald and turquoise, aquamarine and violet. Colours he thought forgotten, colours unknown in the palace. He knew then that his own senses had been fogged, blunted by something.

Sessera, went his mind. It's on the food, it's in the smoke, it's in your dreams…

But not in this dream. This dream was somewhere else, something else. He lifted his eyes away and looked down the long avenues of trees and saw Wincy, still waiting for him.

She beckoned and he went forward to meet her. She took his hand and turned slightly to one side. He turned with her and saw that a fountain shaped like a pair of intertwined dolphins gently splashed, slightly overspilling into a small, perfectly clear pool.

Beyond it stood a silvery pavilion, a summer house with open sides. There were two people seated there, a very old man and an extraordinarily beautiful woman.

There were tall and feathery plants everywhere, twining up the pillars of the summer house, covering the trunks of the trees. Dark moths with velvety wings flitted between the waxy blooms of pale lilies. Somewhere, a bird cried out, a mournful falling note in its song.

Darius hardly noticed how he got there, but suddenly the old man was standing up, looking at him with a keen, measuring gaze, as he went up the steps of the summer house.

"Good," he commented. "Good work, Wincy. Come in, boy, come in." He stood back, letting Darius into the summer house. Darius glanced back over his shoulder in panic and saw Wincy drop a deep curtsey.

Darius hurriedly executed a bow of sorts. He hardly dared look directly at the woman. There was an impression of softness and femininity and the scent of freesia...

Wincy said, "My Lady, this is my cousin Darius, of whom you have heard me speak."

"So I see." The lady's voice was dry. "Well, Darius, how do you like working for my husband?"

"Your hus –?" He stopped, looking her in the face for the first time. She took his breath away. He had never seen a more beautiful woman. This was the Countess Philomena, of course. Wincy was one of her ladies-in-waiting, had been for years.

He became aware that he was staring at the Countess with unbecoming frankness. She was so exquisite, so delicate and her skin seemed flecked with gold. She seemed to shimmer before him. He looked away, furiously aware that he was blushing.

"Well? I asked you a question, Darius." Her voice was now tinged with amusement.

"Very well, my Lady," he stammered.

"Really?"

She was smaller than Wincy, of a fragile build. Her silvery-blonde hair was twisted into an elaborate structure of plaited loops set with pearls and aquamarines. Her eyes were of that green that seems almost blue in the shade. She was wearing an overdress of pale gauze over a green silk sheath. There was something almost brittle about this elegance. She might shatter and break at any moment. She made Darius feel brutish and clumsy.

The old man also wore green, a corduroy suit with foaming lace at the throat and wrists. His eyes were a piercing version of the Countess's, and then Wincy whispered to Darius that this was Lord Dulchimer, the Countess's father.

Again Darius bowed. He felt, quite strongly, that the Countess and her father and this subtle world of greens and blues was where he belonged. This was home. In some confusion he looked again at Wincy and she smiled reassuringly.

"Sit down, Darius," she said, indicating a chair opposite the Countess.

He bowed again. It was easier than speaking.

The Countess's eyes gleamed at him. "You are in my husband's private company, I understand, and have sworn loyalty to him. You will comprehend that there is at present an ... estrangement ... between my husband and myself which I desire to heal. In service of this, I ask you to pledge an equal loyalty to me. I seek nothing more than a reconciliation. To clear my name with him.

132

"There is someone at his court who has planted false evidence against me. My husband has been deliberately misled by my enemies. I do not expect you to do anything about this, to take any risks. I want you to keep your eyes open. To observe what goes on, what is happening. Do you understand how important it is for us to have a friendly soul within the palace?"

"Of course, my Lady." And yet his heart was beating fast, his palms slightly sweaty and uncomfortable. He was being asked to spy. It terrified him.

It was as if she had read his mind. "Of course, we have no desire to put you into the position of spy. All we want is an ally. A friend in the palace. And if you should happen to observe the rotas and movements of the Earl's personal servants, so much the better. When the time comes, I will need to make contact with the Earl once more, and any information at all will be helpful. But you personally will not be involved. My word on this."

Darius swallowed. And then he looked directly at those devastating green eyes and was lost.

He'd do anything for her. Challenge the Earl himself, if necessary. He bowed yet again, the lowest bow he'd ever made. "My Lady," he said, "you may rest assured that I will do my uttermost to serve you."

The pomposity of his words would have driven

Laura to giggles, but he didn't care. This was heroic, the kind of mission he'd read about in ancient romances.

The Countess was taking a diamond pin from her silvery hair and holding it out to him. As if he were a knight from olden days, he took it from her and slipped it into the breast pocket of his shirt.

The green forest faded swiftly back into greyness as he stepped down from the summer house. A whirling sensation, a strange dizziness and then he was whisking along beside Wincy through the city once more, the buildings and streets and temples passing in a blur around them.

He managed to catch his breath long enough to ask Wincy about Laura.

"I don't know," she said. "We've had no news about her or Randall or any of our old friends. In truth, we have not attempted to contact them. There are spies everywhere and we have no intention of leading our friends into danger. Between us, Lord Dulchimer, the Countess and I have managed to set up a protection for this, our joint dreaming. We would be at risk anywhere else. We've lost touch with the other aquemancers. But don't worry about Laura, Darry. She's a clever girl, I'm sure she'll be all right."

"She's just a kid," he said, quite forgetting that he was only minutes older.

Wincy laughed. "You're both brave and re-sourceful and one day will laugh together about all this. Have faith, Darius. Laura will be fine."

And then she was no longer there and he was back in bed, the sheets somewhat rumpled and no sign that water had ever fallen from the beam above.

It had been a dream. He knew it, but that didn't help at all. It had been a true dream, a different concept altogether. The dreaming as a place, a sanctuary...

He was so tired, physically exhausted by the day, mentally by the night. He dreaded the bell which would mean it would start again all too soon, but he couldn't sleep.

The scar on his hand was throbbing painfully. He realized then that it had been hurting all night. He looked at it. The raised lumps of flesh were red and angry-looking.

He thrust it under the cool linen pillow and nearly cried out as a sharp pain jabbed at his thumb. He lifted the pillow and looked beneath it. A diamond pin, something immediately familiar to him. There was a spot of blood on the linen. He sat up in bed for a while holding it in his hand, remembering. Then he stuck it back into the sheet beneath his pillow.

It was lunatic. He'd be caught and executed, like Jethro. How could Wincy put him in such danger? What was she up to?

He tossed and turned for a while.

He had no idea that Perrian had seen all this. He had no idea that Perrian waited patiently until Darius was asleep before himself getting up and creeping from the dormitory.

CHAPTER 12

Max

Laura awoke with a jolt. Randall's hand was on her shoulder. "Sorry, Laura," he said. "Quinland said to bring you along right away."

In the candlelight, Randall looked shocking, his face drawn with lines, deep dark shadows beneath the eyes. "We've been up all night," he said. "We went through those bottles you chose. Of the twenty-three, twelve were aquemancers." He smiled at her, tiredly. "It's been quite a night. Congratulations, cousin. I misjudged you. I thought you were just a kid, a nuisance. You're the bee's knees with Quinland. He wants you to pick out another selection."

"Of course!" Laura was thrilled. To have an

important, crucial skill like that! To have Randall apologize! "But you didn't find Wincy?"

He shook his head. "Quin's beginning to wonder if she's been found already."

"Surely she'd get in touch?" She was pulling on her boots and splashing water on her face as they spoke.

"Yes. That's what keeps us going, of course. Wincy and all those other water-witches. They're out there somewhere. Look, here's some breakfast." He handed her a heavy cake-like pastry filled with spicy apricots.

She was ravenous. He watched her eat with amusement. "Ready?" he asked when she'd finished. He gave her a bag to sling over one shoulder, in case they found anything on the way. Then it was out into the burning street once more.

"Things are hotting up and I don't mean the temperature," said Randall as they passed yet another band of soldiers in fiery orange uniforms. Laura hated the way their bronze helmets concealed their faces. It made them look inhuman, she thought.

They were stopped once, but Randall put on a whiny voice, holding out his thin hand like some poor half-wit, begging for alms. Laura kept her eyes down, mumbling unintelligibly. They were allowed to pass.

The burning torches were still alight, although it

was now daylight. The sickly smoke still hung in the air. Laura wondered what would happen if a fire started, given that a majority of the buildings in Bricus appeared to be made of wood.

Every now and then her eyes caught on the glint of glass. But only occasionally was it a bottle with liquid inside. Most of their finds came from the alleyways beside inns and restaurants. By the time they reached the curtain of ivy, their bags were only half full.

Quinland met them at the entrance. He immediately took Laura's hands and kissed her. His eyes were gleaming. "Well, you marvellous girl, twelve aquemancers owe their freedom to you!" He was thrilled with her but she could also see that he was exhausted.

"Do we really need to go on now, Quinland? You and Randall look so tired." She sounded so confident, even to herself.

"Just like your cousin Wincy," said Quinland fondly. "Actually, we want you to spend the morning going through the shelves in here, seeing what you can find, while we have a quick nap. Max and Nina will keep you company. With any luck, you'll have found enough to keep us going all afternoon and evening."

Already her eyes were scanning the rows of bottles in the hallway, the rows of bottles on the dim stairs. Almost unthinkingly her hand reached out and took down a tiny cut glass perfume flask. And then a yellow-tinged chemist's flagon caught her attention. A little further on a plain bottle on the floor by the skirting board reminded her immediately of one of the bottles Wincy had sent her when she was ten. It called to her as strongly as if it had a voice. It could not be left there, it demanded to be taken up. Wordlessly she handed them to Randall, who was following after her.

By the time they reached the central chamber both he and Quinland had their arms full. Max and Nina were sprawled on the cushions in the butler's pantry, fast asleep. Laura helped Randall put the bottles down on the small table. Then he unkindly clapped his hands together and the two sleepers jumped.

"Come on, you two. Work to do!"

Max opened one eye. "You're just jealous," he said. He uncurled, stretching like a cat against the soft cushions. Nina was rubbing her eyes like a sleepy child.

"So, our star has arrived," she said. "Does this mean it's back to the grindstone?"

"For goodness' sake!" Randall snapped.

"Sorry," said Nina, although she didn't sound in the least regretful.

"She's always awful before breakfast," said Max.

"I know. That's why I brought these," said

Randall, unfolding a paper napkin on the table. It contained two more of the apricot pasties, their cinnamon scent filling the enclosed chamber.

"Treats!" said Nina, falling on them.

"Well, we've got something to celebrate," said Quinland tiredly. "Twelve friends released, twelve allies active once more." He had already subsided on to the cushions, yawning. "Wake me up in two hours," he said. On the other side of the chamber, Randall was already stretching out his long length.

"Sweet dreams," said Nina, but they were already asleep.

Max was looking at the table. "You've chosen these already?"

She nodded. "I haven't even started in here though," she said. "And there are all those other rooms."

"How do you know which ones to choose?"

"Wincy used to send me bottles as presents when I was little. The ones I've chosen here remind me of them, something in the shape or the colour or the etching..." She shrugged. "It's nothing I could explain logically."

They passed into the hallway.

"What's up there?" Laura asked.

"More of the same," said Max. A pause. He looked at her. "It's endless, you know, this hunting of witches. I don't know if we'll ever find them all, even with your help. Bricus is full of bottles and there were so many fugitives." He walked away from her, picking up a small square-shouldered blue flask. "There was an attack from the palace, using fireflies, soon after the Pyromancer Lerris arrived in Bricus. All the aquemancers were rounded up. It happened in the space of a few hours. I expect Randall has told you about this already. Our parents tried to transform." He was speaking quietly, holding the bottle up to the light, squinting against the glow from the candelabra. "It happened not far from here, in our family home. Randall was there, too. A firefly had burned down the door, it was coming for us. It was desperate... We thought the transformation had worked, but something went wrong... The firefly got in the way. I don't think our parents ever made it into the dreaming."

The old house soared above them, filled with glassy echoes, empty passages where the bottles waited in serried ranks, green, gold and amber, stretching away into deserted bedrooms and attics.

She shivered. "Are you sure? Perhaps they'll be waiting somewhere –"

"Understand, Laura, I think it's useless." He turned to face her, his eyes deeply serious. "We lost the water, the link. It evaporated under the firefly's breath. We'll never find them again."

"Max –"

"So, I suggest that Nina and I do the preliminary tests on these while you have a go up there."

For a moment she looked at him, recognizing the tension that kept his words so even, so distant.

"All right," she agreed at last. What else could she do? She looked at the massed colours of glass surrounding them. It had felt like a game, up to this. But now she felt daunted by the numbers, the brightness, the weight of the responsibility.

But as she began to wander through the house, through those empty, dusty rooms, where the wood was warm beneath her fingers, the glass cool, she relaxed and let her hands wander towards the shelves and tables and sideboards.

In what seemed like no time at all she had found another two dozen bottles. Max accompanied her for much of this, and at the same time she discovered that Max and Nina were brother and sister. Wincy and Randall had been close friends of their parents and had adopted them. Like Quinland and Randall, Max and Nina shared an almost fanatical devotion to Wincy.

She started up the stairs, fascinated by the flickering colours of the candlelight reflected through glass. All the colours of the rainbow were there, crowding at her. And every now and then, sensing that clear, high note of longing, she took one down.

It was impossible to tell what called her. It was

like a sound, a voice, but she knew she was hearing nothing. Something seemed to vibrate, making a resonance for her to respond to. The whole house seemed full of unheard voices clamouring for her attention.

But after a while she sighed. Her arms were full and besides she wasn't sure that she was picking it up clearly any more. She went back downstairs to the kitchen and Max helped her unload on the table. He and Nina had processed a long line of bottles and a group of some thirty or so stood by the fire, ready for Quin and Randall to examine.

The room was stuffy, airless and hot. She suddenly felt weary.

"Can't we go and get some fresh air?" she said. "I could do with a break."

"Fair enough." Max picked up a ragged cloak from a chair. "Coming, Nina?"

She shook her head. "I'll tell Quinland where you are. You'll stay near the market, won't you?"

"Of course."

It was a mistake.

The burning streets did not feel much better than the house. The air was harsh and dry and Laura smelled sweat and rotting vegetables and charred meat from the stalls. A throng of people crushed against them. The bright colours of their clothes struck her as cheap and gaudy.

And there was something else, an acrid stink that reminded her of the smoke that had billowed everywhere the day before. "What *is* that smell?" she said to Max, wrinkling her nose.

"I think – but I hope I'm wrong – that it's a firefly. They always stink."

Laura shuddered. She'd never seen a firefly before. "Don't they need a pyromancer to control them?" she asked nervously.

He nodded. "There'll be one around somewhere." He took her arm. "Let's get out of this. Quin will be ready soon—"

"*Who* did you say?" A man to Max's right swung round suddenly and Laura saw the flash of scarlet beneath his cloak. He'd seized Max by the shoulder. Too late she saw the blazing dragon crest on his chest. She turned and ran, but a soldier stepped out of the crowd and grabbed her. She wriggled and bit at the hand that held her. The man cursed, bringing his other hand sharply down on the side of her face. The sudden pain stunned her. She staggered.

As if by magic the crowds had withdrawn. Laura and Max were surrounded only by soldiers and the Pyromancer's visor was turned towards them.

"Tell me," he invited. "Was that Quinland the Aquemancer you were discussing?"

"Who, sir? No, sir," Max mumbled. He looked

both stupid and scared. Like someone quite different. "My aunty Queenie, that's who…"

The Pyromancer wasn't listening. He turned to Laura.

Watching Max's transformation, she decided to follow suit. It was a tactic Randall used, after all. Surely it wasn't that difficult?

But her head ached from the blow and she knew she wasn't thinking clearly.

The Pyromancer was looking closely at her. "A girl," he said, "disguised as a boy. Now, why?" He spoke softly, as if to himself.

"Sir, it's not safe for a woman to live in the streets," she said.

"True enough. But why do I think there's more to this? Now, what have you here?" His gloved hands darted out and seized the bottle she'd tucked into her jacket pocket.

Another of those long, faceless glances again, searching her face for some clue. She tried to keep her expression blank.

The Pyromancer nodded minutely to the soldier who held her and she was aware that the man's hand was moving from her shoulder to the side of her neck. His fingers tightened. There was a feeling of pressure thumping through her head, of black spots in her vision growing and spreading together until there was nothing but black, everywhere.

CHAPTER 13

Firefly

"They left us there." Max looked at Quinland in puzzlement. Laura was sitting at the table, her elbows on her knees, her head dropped between her hands.

Max was dishevelled, dark hair falling over his left eye where a bruise was rapidly forming. "I don't know what happened. They suddenly lost interest. I saw Laura fall to the ground and there was a bit of a fight. Then it all went black. When we woke up we were both in one of the side alleys of the market."

Quinland was frowning. "Are you sure that's *all* that happened? You've not missed anything, any details?"

Laura remembered the way the Pyromancer had taken the bottle from her. She sat up, her hand flying to her pocket.

"It's all right," said Randall calmly. "I put your bottle on the table with the others."

Looking across the room at the table through blurry eyes, Laura couldn't remember which one it was. Was it the sloping-shouldered wine bottle? Or the square medicine flask? She really had no idea. Yellowish, she thought. Or brown.

What did it matter? Her head hurt and she felt obscurely like crying. She really, really needed to see Darius and talk to him. She missed him so much. It was like trying to operate with one sense missing, as if she was crippled in some way. There was no one to discuss everything with, no one to share all her experiences, to make her see them in that off-centre, amused, twinnish perspective. Randall and Quinland and Max were all very well, and she liked them all, but it wasn't the same…

She became aware that Max was watching her. "Sorry," he said. "We shouldn't have gone out."

"You weren't to know," said Quinland. He didn't look that much better for his rest.

"They're trying to force it," said Randall. He too looked tense and nervy. "A confrontation. They must be very confident."

"Except we're twelve stronger than we were

this time yesterday," said Quinland, cheering up. He was smiling at Laura again and she felt encouraged. "And who knows what we may find today? You rest here, Laura, and watch what we make of this batch."

He gestured towards the crowded table. Randall picked up a bottle from it and they began.

Nothing with the first. Or with the second. Laura began to wonder if her skill had deserted her. But everyone adjourned to the butler's pantry for the third and a powerful-looking woman with wild red hair emerged. She fluttered her devastating black eyelashes at Randall and ran her hand languorously over his cheek before drifting from the house in wafting, silky layers of chiffon.

The fourth bottle revealed a teenage lad not much older than Laura. He skipped and jumped over the cushions as if he'd been coiled up like a spring in a box. He bounded over to Laura and kissed her full on the lips.

"For ever yours, dear lady," he crowed, before bounding out down the hallway. They heard the front door bang, and all the bottles rattled as the house shook.

Quinland permitted himself a small smile. "Tamlin." He shrugged. "Never changes. *Not* the most useful of enchanters, but someone you'd miss, especially at parties."

They'd started on the next bottle before Laura

realized that it was the one the Pyromancer had taken from her.

"That's the one –" she began, but Randall held up his hand, frowning. He didn't want her to interrupt Quinland's concentration. He was already sitting quietly, his hands cradling the golden bowl as if it were made of gold leaf.

Nina was there too, her eyes sparkling with excitement. She took Laura by the hand. "Come and sit here," she said, indicating a bench half concealed behind a curtain. "You can see really clearly and we won't distract them."

So Laura crept round the back of the pantry and sat with Nina. She found herself drawn into Quinland's stillness, her thoughts quietening, steadying. She was faintly aware of his unvoiced incantation.

Absorbed in this, she did not at first notice the mist coalescing above the golden dish. It wavered and flickered there, reflecting something of the gold colour of the dish itself.

Laura leaned forward, trying to make out what manner of aquemancer would emerge. The orangey tinge to it became more pronounced. Another red-haired witch, she wondered?

Then, without warning, the gold mist exploded. A blaze of heat hit out at them. Laura and Nina were knocked backwards off their bench by the force of it. One of the curtains was immediately engulfed in flames. The air was full of the smell of burning and someone was screaming and Laura only had a moment to register what had happened.

A firefly: it had to be. She'd never seen one before, but what other creature could cause such instant devastation? It was Nina who had screamed, but Laura was too shaken, too breathless to cry out. She could not drag her eyes away from the sight. A creature of fire and light darted out into the kitchen, and it seemed as unstable as lightning, jerking and flaring and with every movement sparks scattered all around it. The kitchen table was smouldering. Flames were sprouting everywhere. Already the cushions and hangings in the pantry were nothing more than charred rags.

On the other side of the kitchen she saw Randall stagger backwards, crashing into a shelf of bottles. Glass shattered all over him.

And the screaming began.

Those bottles must have held the way through for more than a few aquemancers. Their frantic wails split through the air.

Nina was pulling on her hand. Laura turned and almost didn't recognize her friend. A stranger stared at her, her face blackened by the scorching flames, her eyebrows and eyelashes non-existent.

And then there was Quinland, scrambling to his feet and staggering out of the pantry. He flung himself across the floor to the sink and grasped a pitcher of water which stood there.

He turned, ready to hurl it at the monster, but the creature was leaping through the air towards him, its fiery wings spreading wide, sweeping along the shelves of bottles.

More crashing glass, more devastation. The firefly was screeching, a weird high-pitched sound, and there were all those other sounds too, howling, weeping ... other aquemancers disappearing into nothingness, screaming down the wild dimensions, losing themselves in dream and nightmare, their only grip on reality shattered.

The force of the noise was immense. The pitcher fell from Quinland's grasp and smashed against the tiles. He dropped to his knees, frantically scooping at the water.

The firefly screamed at him and a jet of flame seared through the air. Quinland fell sideways, and as his shoulder hit the tiled floor, he hurled the water, those few drops, at the firefly.

It flinched, suddenly backing off, as if those few drops were made of acid. It was flustered, and its spiky wings became tangled in the charred curtains. For a moment it hung there, battering against the black rags, snarling.

Laura and Nina edged round the wall towards the hallway, mesmerized by what was happening. It looked as if Quinland had the answer, but how to get more water? There was smoke everywhere, billowing from the remains of the cushions. She could not see what Randall was doing, she had no idea where Max was...

Quinland flicked a glance at them. "Get *out* of here!" he yelled. Nina was pulling on Laura's arm, forcing her into the hall, although she felt desperate about what was happening to Randall and Max.

The smoke clouds were dense and vicious-smelling. Both girls were choking, their eyes running.

Somehow they managed to stumble into the long corridor. Laura hung back, feeling that she shouldn't leave, she should try to help –

"Leave it. There's nothing we can do." Nina kept up the pressure.

"He – Quin needs more water," Laura gasped. "And where's Randall? Max?"

"Here." Another figure stumbled through the smoke towards her. Max, with a bucket of water. She had no idea where he could have got it from. She didn't see what happened next, because Nina had pulled her further along the corridor towards the street door.

"We can't leave them!" Laura cried.

"We need help! More water!" And saying that, Nina pulled aside the curtain of ivy and they were out in the street.

* * *

It was midday, the sun scorching down overhead, the market filled with the usual stinking, sweaty crowds. Laura gasped in great lungfuls of dirty, stinking pollution as if it were the purest, sweetest mountain air. She'd been suffocating in there.

Then, only then, did she really take in what Nina looked like. Aside from the blackened skin, her clothes were all scorched and hanging in shreds. "Are you all right?" she asked, shocked.

"Are *you*?"

Laura realized that she must look much the same. But they had more important things to worry about than their appearance.

Clouds of smoke still billowed from behind the ivy screen. Nina ran to a passer-by. "There's a fire in there!" she shouted, pointing. "We need water, lots of water, there are still people in there –"

They were in luck. The man was cool and efficient and soon a chain of people passing buckets from a pump was organized. It seemed to take ages, but at last the smoke died away and there were no more leaping flames. Together with several townspeople, Nina and Laura picked their way through the blackened, stifling hallway, their boots crunching on the broken glass.

There was hardly a single bottle left whole. But the noise had died, there was no further sound of screaming or despair.

"Max? Quin?" they called, turning over the damp frail debris. But there was no sound at all, beyond the crunch of their steps on glass and the squelch of water in their boots.

Water. The ground floor of the house was swimming with it. There was no sign of any of the men.

"Might Quinland and Randall have used one of those watery transformations?" Laura asked Nina.

She nodded, tight-lipped. "They'll have found a way into some neat little hideaway. If the firefly didn't get them first, *they'll* be all right."

"Max?" Laura whispered.

"He wouldn't do that. It would mean leaving me behind." And all at once her face seemed to collapse and crumple and Laura saw tears falling over her cheeks. Her shoulders convulsed. Laura held her close and felt her own tears start. What if Darius had been caught here, burning up like a fly in an oven? But it wasn't only that she felt sympathy because of Darius. She had been moved by Max, by the account of what had happened to his and Nina's parents. She cared.

"There's someone here." It was the efficient man who spoke, turning over the remains of the cushions. He was bending over a shapeless heap on the floor. "He's alive!"

On her knees beside the figure, Nina was crying again, this time with relief.

It was Max.

* * *

The man who had found Max was by trade an apothecary and gave them lotions and bandages and helped them bind up the worst of his wounds. There were terrible burns down his left arm and shoulder. Even the left side of his face was red and shiny, although the apothecary said that wasn't serious. It was Max's left forearm which really worried them, and although he was conscious, they could see that the pain of it was almost more than he could bear.

The apothecary, whose name was Milo, helped them get Max back to Silver Street. They waved goodbye to him at the end of the Street, not wanting to give away Randall's hideaway.

Between them they managed to guide Max through the garden and into the shed. The trap-door and steeply slanting stairs were a different matter, because it was clear that Max could not bear to be touched. They had to stand by, watching as he slowly and painfully limped down the stairway.

He slumped against the wall at the bottom for a moment, hiding his face from them. Then Nina stepped forward and very gently helped him over to the couch where Laura had been sleeping. He lay down and Nina quickly measured out some of the medicine Milo had given them.

He waved it away.

"Do take it, Max, it'll help you sleep."

"Can't afford to sleep. Not yet. Listen." For a moment he stopped, trying to gather his strength. "Nina – Laura – one of you has to go back to Quin's place. He and Randall are both there, I saw it happen. In the pantry, by the door, two small glass phials – God knows whether those clod-hopping firefighters crushed them or not – but you'll have to find them…"

He stopped, his voice trailing away. Laura had poured water from the jug on the table and he drank a little. "You'll have to take care. I threw water all over that firefly, and I think I got it all, but they have been known to self-ignite… Take water with you, take care…"

His head fell back and Nina gave a small moan of anxiety. Laura felt for Max's pulse, as she had seen Milo do. It was there, weak and tremulous, but very definitely there.

"I can't leave him," said Nina, bleakly.

"I know," Laura said. She was already looking round for some kind of receptacle. There was a leather-bound flask over a hook by the door. She filled it with water, sketched a hasty goodbye to Nina and went back out into the street.

CHAPTER 14

On Guard

"You'll be on active duty tomorrow," said the Captain. "A chance to show off some of these hard-won skills."

Darius and his colleagues were standing to attention after the evening session. They were tired, longing for bed. But this was news to make them all alert.

At last. Real work.

But Darius had more complicated responses. He'd spent all day worrying about what Wincy and the Countess had told him. He'd found himself wondering exactly what it meant, to keep his eyes open on their behalf, but he'd actually seen no sign of the Earl that day and anyway

Perrian had stuck like a leech to him, leaving him with no free time at all.

He was rather flattered by this. Perrian was so much better than he was at all the physical tasks. He always won every wrestling bout, every trial of strength. And even when it came to memorizing texts, Perrian had a parrot-like facility. He always knew all the answers, although he never showed off. He was quiet, although no one could mistake it for shyness, and Darius was aware that no one else knew who Perrian's father was. Perrian never confided in anyone but Darius and even Darius had no idea how much he knew about aquemancy; whether Perrian knew what the Earl's Guard did with all this skill, all this discipline. Did he know about the executions? Did he share the hatred of water-witches?

The Captain was still talking. He announced that a number of witches had been reported to the Pyromancer. It seemed that some of them had returned to Bricus, from wherever they had been hiding. Darius held his breath. Certain premises had already been searched, but no one had been found there. The Pyromancer wanted those premises watched, in case the inhabitants attempted to return, while other places were searched.

"The intention is to root out the Earl's enemies, traitors to the state. It is time to establish the undisputed supremacy of the Pyromancy over these unruly elements," said the Captain, frowning at the cadets. "It is now your turn to show that your training has not been wasted. Time to prove your loyalty."

It was only then that Darius thought to look at the Earl, seated far away from them at the end of the hall beneath a portrait of a beautiful woman. There was a tall figure draped in cloth-of-gold, sunburst helmet glinting in the candlelight. Was it merely a trick of that same shimmering light that made it seem that the Earl's eyes were glowing? Certainly, Darius had never seen him look so alien before.

If he hadn't known better, if the whole idea was not inconceivable and preposterous, Darius would have sworn that the Earl's mind had been possessed by fire.

Perrian was enthralled. "Real work at last," he said with satisfaction. He and Darius were stationed with a squadron of soldiers in a corner of the market. Behind them some creepers and ivy had been ripped away from a wall and the door standing open there was scarred by flame.

The house they were guarding had been gutted by fire. They were standing rigidly to attention outside the door, their backs to the gaping black tunnel which led into the house. They were directly under the midday sun, their eyes watchfully scanning the crowds through the visors of their helmets.

In the mass of people, the ever-changing shapes of the crowd took all their attention. They didn't even notice the urchin lingering behind the barrows of the fruit merchants, carefully observing the observers for more than an hour.

They were irritated when the urchin started pelting them with rotten tomatoes, but they were trained to stand still and take it. Neither of them moved.

But then other children joined in the game. No one made any attempt to stop them: instead, the market people laughed and applauded whenever a direct hit was scored.

"I'll slaughter that kid if I ever get my hands on him," said Darius vengefully. Overripe tomato flesh was dripping down the visor of his helmet. He could hardly see anything.

Perrian was furious. "Let's stop this. It makes us look such fools." He glanced at Darius. "You stay here. I'll take some of the men and put a stop to it." He marched sternly towards the crowd, his sword in his hand, followed by six or seven soldiers.

Darius dashed away the tomato from his visor. So much for dignity. He watched Perrian and the men fling the vegetable stall over, scattering aubergines and peppers and beans and olives in the dust.

There was of course no sign of the original urchin, but Perrian gave the stallkeeper a light tap with the flat of his sword when he complained. The man, a beefy six-footer with a ruddy face, wasn't taking treatment like that. He took a wild swing at Perrian, who had no difficulty blocking it. "Right!" Darius heard him shout. "You're under arrest. Assaulting a member of the Earl's own cadet force –"

The man laughed and made a lewd gesture and a comment about whippersnappers, and the crowd giggled. Darius couldn't believe how Perrian was mishandling all this. He saw a couple of the soldiers hanging back from it all, and recognized one of them as Franklin. Time to bring some order to this: he strode across the market place towards the melée and didn't notice the urchin slip into the doorway as soon as his back was turned.

Nothing had changed. Broken glass still crunched beneath Laura's feet; pools of water reflected only darkness. In the light of the torch she had brought with her she saw that only a few bottles remained intact on the shelves. She felt drawn to none of them. The bleak vaulting hollow of the stairwell echoed above her. She moved quickly, knowing that she had only a few minutes before the guards returned to their post.

There was glass everywhere in the kitchen, and it was still dark there. The shutters remained in place over the window. In the torchlight, she could see that the hangings and cushions were ripped and scorched. In the centre of the mess a black slug-like sticky substance was smeared over the rags. It stank. Laura put her hand over her nose, trying not to gag.

She could see no intact bottles anywhere. Nothing resembling perfume flasks. She squatted down, bringing the torch close to the floor, and began to pick over the ragged remains.

The door down the hallway suddenly banged. At the same moment she glimpsed the complicated glinting of cut glass and scooped up the tiny glass bottle half concealed under the enormous iron range.

There were footsteps coming down the hallway towards the kitchen. In a panic she whirled round, looking for somewhere to hide.

She needed to extinguish the torch. Without thinking she jammed it downwards into the sticky blackness in the centre of the floor.

The stink was appalling, a sudden and overwhelming waft of sulphur fumes. Laura dived behind the remaining shreds of curtain, trying to breathe through her mouth.

The torch spluttered and fizzed and went out, although the smell of sulphur continued to strengthen. In the darkness she heard voices, and nearly forgot all caution.

Darius. Darius's voice coming towards her, shouting, "Get a torch, Franklin, I can't see anything –"

And then an explosion, the sound and light coming from nowhere and blazing. The chamber was instantaneously filled with light. The stinking black mess had ignited like oil, flaring up into a shape that Laura knew would give her nightmares for ever.

Claws and wings, and that horrible scaly head. Its right leg was still fastened into the black gunge and one of its wings was broken, hanging limply.

A firefly, partially revived by Laura's torch... Darius was shouting something indistinguishable, and she could see him now in the light emanating from the flickering monster between them.

But his face was disguised by that strange helmet and she wondered, in the midst of all the heat and light and fear, whether this really was her beloved twin brother. He was backing towards the hall, his sword drawn, making useless swipes at the ferociously flaring monster.

There was nothing she could do. The glass phial in her pocket reminded her that she needed to find one more. Glancing up towards the firefly, she fell to her knees, scrabbling among the ruined cushions.

The firefly had not noticed her. All its attention was taken by Darius and she wanted desperately to distract it. But behind her there was only a blank wall, whereas Darius at least had the means to retreat.

The firefly suddenly breathed out a vast plume of flame, like a demented firework. It scorched through the air directly at Darius's head.

She screamed then, but it was not Darius who received the force of the blast. She saw her brother thrust aside by another uniformed figure, a stranger she did not recognize. It was this stranger who received the blazing lick of flame.

She saw him fall to the ground, and as he fell the bucket of water he was carrying splashed all over the firefly. It howled, a dreadful scraping noise like nails on a blackboard, as the billowing clouds of heated gas collapsed in on themselves. It shrank as she watched, shrivelling and squealing like a stuck pig, until there was nothing left but that repellent sticky black mess on the floor.

She saw Darius bend down beside the burned soldier, lifting him gently in his arms and stumbling back down the hallway to the market place.

She wanted more than anything to run after him. She wanted to say, "Darry, it's me, where have you been? What's happened to you?"

But he looked so strange in that visored helmet and brilliant uniform that her words dried up. Was that really him? She couldn't understand what had happened. She didn't know what to say, how to begin...

"Darry?" It came out as no more than a squeak and he didn't even turn round. But something caught her eye as he went through the door. A glint of glass, the second perfume bottle, wedged into the corner between door and wall. She thrust it into her pocket and when she looked up again, Darius had gone.

So she had let him go, her brother in his flashy uniform of scarlet with the golden dragon motif.

Not a dragon motif. It was a firefly, embroidered on his uniform, on the uniform of all the soldiers.

She waited until long after his footsteps had disappeared into silence. And then she nervously picked her way through the glass-strewn mess. She avoided the black stuff with a shudder.

She crept away from Quinland's ruined hide-away back to Silver Street, clutching in her hand the two tiny bottles she hoped would reveal her friends.

CHAPTER 15

Franklin

Darius waited outside the sick bay, nervously twining the strap of his helmet over and over in his hands.

No one had given him any news. He knew that Franklin was still alive, or why else would the doctor still be in there, bent over that burned body? But no one had told him what Franklin's chances were.

His friend had been scorched, charred like meat on a grill. Darius was horrified by what had happened to him. And he'd never seen anything like that firefly, that ferocious, evil, glowing creature of flame. Or had he? There was something lurking in his mind, some memory of a nightmare or dream. He'd seen that long-nosed head before, those blank, inimical features...

But he couldn't remember where or when. In all those weeks of training, no one had mentioned fireflies to him. And so he had no protection against it, no way of knowing that there was a comparatively simple and effective defence.

Franklin had known, Franklin had come to his rescue with that bucket of water. Darius owed his life to Franklin, one of the conscripts who hadn't made it out of the ranks.

"Are you all right?"

He looked up into Jasper's eyes. "*I'm* fine," he said miserably. "But Franklin –" He stopped, remembering that Perrian's father was a Senior, close to the Earl himself, not someone to care overmuch what had happened to an ordinary soldier.

The older man shrugged. "He'll be OK, they say. A few scars perhaps, but so what? Injury comes with the job."

It seemed very cool to Darius. Was this how professionals behaved?

Jasper sat down beside Darius. "We need to know more details of all this, of course."

"Franklin saved my life," Darius said.

Jasper ignored it. "You'll have to write a detailed report for the record. It's very unusual to find a firefly out of control. Something must have gone wrong." He frowned. "The Earl wants to see you after supper. Present yourself in his study. And get yourself cleaned up. You're a disgrace like that."

But his eyes were kind. He stood up, and for a moment his hand rested on Darius's shoulder. "Don't you worry too much about Franklin Laclos. People get hurt in our profession. As I said, it's part of the job."

"I know. My father was a soldier too." Darius stopped. He could hardly remember his father at all.

"Franklin's a street boy. There's no one to worry about him," said Jasper reassuringly. He strode off down the corridor, leaving Darius with thoughts too complicated to express.

"Broken glass, you say? All over the floor?"

"Yes, sir. Thousands of bottles, all different sorts, smashed everywhere. It looked like there had been a fight."

"And the hangings were scorched." The Pyromancer nodded with satisfaction, his countenance unknowable behind the visored helmet. The Earl was lounging back in one of the leather armchairs in the study, watching Darius's interrogation with lazy attention.

"It must have been an aquemancer's den," said the Pyromancer to the Earl, who nodded slowly.

Marrin had not once taken his eyes from Darius's face.

The Pyromancer returned to his questions. "You had been stationed outside the house all morning and yet you saw no signs of the firefly?"

"No, sir. The place was empty when we arrived, we checked it over. But –" Darius stopped.

"Go on." The Pyromancer spoke sharply.

"We were diverted. There was a fight in the market place and I went to help Perrian…"

"You left your post?" The Earl sat up.

"Sir, they were *laughing* at us!"

"What does the laughter of fools matter?" The Earl banged his fist down on the arm of his chair. "Your orders were to guard the doorway. Not to brawl in the streets."

"Sir!" Darius was white-faced.

"And your friend has paid a high price for his impetuosity." Marrin stood up and crossed the room to where Darius stood miserably in the centre of a richly-woven rug. "It's hard, I know," he said softly. "And we all have to learn somehow. Genuine learning, real learning always hurts, of course. You'll never leave your post now, will you?" He stared into Darius's eyes, and Darius couldn't look away, although he wanted to. There was fire at the back of the Earl's eyes, a raging furnace of madness.

But his words gave no inkling of it. "But still,

you must now realize what happened. Someone must have entered the hideout while you were off maintaining your precious dignity. Someone who managed to release a firefly…"

"A pyromancer?" Darius dared.

"No." This from the Pyromancer himself. "No. I would have known. However, there is another explanation. I have … practised a little aquemancy myself. Since finding a way in, I have spent some little time exploring the dreaming, and have some skills in that area. I have placed there several fireflies, to be discovered by our meddlesome aquemancers. There are fireflies bound to bottles here and there throughout the city. In fact, I placed a firefly in the dreaming only the other day, and gave the bottle back to an urchin in the market place… That is what must have happened today. The urchin was clearly in league with aquemancers. Someone attempted to release a water-witch from it, in that room near the market. Think, boy!" The Pyromancer's voice hissed through the air. "You had an aquemancer in that building and you never even knew it. You let him or her go."

Darius could say nothing. The Earl had released him from that unnerving stare. He hung his head in shame.

"Didn't you see anyone? Didn't you notice *anything*?"

Darius shook his head. He was confused and depressed. He didn't understand any of this. There was just the knowledge that he had failed. He had failed Franklin, and the Earl, and Wincy...

Wincy. And the Countess. How could he have forgotten them? In all the excitement, all the tension of the day's events, he had not thought once of his strange midnight encounter.

His thoughts were a mess. He could make no sense of it all. He needed to know more, more about aquemancers, and the Earl and fireflies and pyromancers. There were too many gaps in his understanding. He tried to bring some order to it all by sticking with what had actually happened. He said, "It all happened so quickly. That creature just ... sprang into life. It was so bright, I couldn't see anything else."

"Dazzled, were you? By its brilliance?" The hissing in the Pyromancer's voice was stronger now and ran through Darius's thoughts, confusing and disruptive. Again, that memory of a dream, something that he had experienced long ago, in another place, another time.

"Sir, I could hardly see anything. And it was coming towards me. It was then that Franklin pushed me out of the way. I fell backwards. I didn't see what happened next."

"What did you think of the firefly?" The Pyromancer's sibilant voice was quiet.

He remembered that flashing, unstable pattern of fire and light, the absolute terror it inspired. He could not frame words around this experience, but some of it must have shown in his face, because the Pyromancer came closer to him, reaching out for his hand. His gloved touch was cool and dry. He said,

"Darius Alderwood Brooke. An Alderwood... Yes, I know your name. You signed it, in full, on your exam paper. Why do you think I had you promoted? You are someone I might use. Don't be afraid. We need a little information from you."

"What information?" His voice, through all the bewilderment, was hardly more than a whisper. Where did his loyalty lie, who was he?

The Pyromancer was still speaking. "Yes, we have always known your connection with aquemancy. In the sacred smoke, you revealed yourself, you opened to us your soul, your secret thoughts. You are Darius Alderwood Brooke, child of Cytheria Alderwood, and cousin to Wincesta Alderwood. The scent of water magic hangs round you, although you yourself are no adept."

He came a little nearer and it was all Darius could do to prevent himself stepping backwards. "We've been watching you, Darius Alderwood Brooke."

It was indescribably chilling. And then that

picture again, suddenly flashing through Darius's mind, Jethro trying to escape, and being run through. He felt his heart beating so loud that he thought the Pyromancer must hear it.

"And yet, let us consider." The Pyromancer's voice was calm. "You have sworn allegiance to the Earl, you wear his mark on your hand..." He paused, and Darius was uneasily aware of the spicy scent that always hung round the Pyromancer's swirling cloth-of-gold cloak.

"Let us consider the phenomenon of the firefly, Darius. You saw a firefly released, out of control, running wild. Without care or skill or knowledge, a firefly was unleashed in that house and no wonder there was destruction. Fireflies feed off men. Didn't you know? And not only their flesh."

Darius could feel the Pyromancer's sickly sweet breath, hot on his face. But he didn't dare flinch, he didn't dare do anything other than stand there, stiffly to attention, while the Earl's Pyromancer spoke to him in sibilant tones.

"There is a relationship between men and fireflies. If a firefly consumes enough, incinerates a number of humans, it begins to take on human shape. Did you know that, Darius? Fireflies are embryo humans, and yet human is not quite the right word for it. Those of us who were fireflies are now somewhat *more* than human...

"It is a two-way process. Men who take the

174

spice, sessera, consistently and over a period of time, begin the transformation the other way. They too become more than human, with abilities you can only begin to imagine.

"It is all because of the spice sessera."

The Pyromancer's hands went to the phial round his neck and tipped a few grains of crimson sand into his gloved hands. "Have you thought about water, boy? About the way it sneaks into our lives, running through our houses, fouling our streets, all the time changing everything it touches, diluting, spoiling, staining... Think on the insidious, creeping evil of water magic."

And as he spoke, the crimson grains of sand stirred with his breath and drifted through the air to settle on Darius's face, on his skin and eyelids and beneath his nose.

He said, "Are all aquemancers evil?" thinking of Wincy and the Countess and the water-witches he saw in his youth, creating their bright rainbows and marvellous fountains.

He remembered, with fire-inspired brilliance, the dolphin fountain by the summer house in his dream.

The Pyromancer's voice continued. "What do you know of aquemancers, Darius? How often have you met with them, what have you told them?"

The hot dry breath of the Pyromancer forced the

spice into his lungs. His limbs felt heavy as lead. Darius was tired, weary of trying to make sense of it all. His eyelids were dropping, and his head rolled on his shoulders.

He dreamed then that the Pyromancer was joined by his friend Perrian. He saw Perrian lift the helmet from the Pyromancer's shoulders and that the dragon head of a firefly breathed its destructive life into him.

His thoughts were lost in dreams of golden fire.

CHAPTER 16

Betrayal

Laura put the two cut-glass bottles down on the table. She had returned to Silver Street to find Nina pacing up and down the narrow space, while Max was drifting in and out of an uneasy sleep. Laura was in a state of shock. She had found her brother, but she'd let him go. She had made no serious attempt to talk to him, she had been too frightened.

Nina had shrugged. "There's nothing you can do about Darius. We can't risk trying to contact the Earl's Guard, it would only draw attention to us."

"Darius would never give us away!"

"How do you know? Have you ever been separated before?"

"No. But you'd always trust Max, wouldn't you? You're his sister, of course you would! It's just like that with twins, only worse. Nina, I have to find a way of seeing him! You must help me!" She was feeling desperate with loneliness.

Nina shook her head. "No. First, we need to release Randall and Quin. Then, only then, when we've got their backup, can we afford to try and contact your brother. Can't you understand? It's vital we get this right…"

"Why is it so difficult? How come everyone can disappear into the dreaming at the drop of a hat and no one can get out again without help?"

"Think about it. You fall asleep easily, don't you? Everyone slips into dreams effortlessly. People even say that things are 'like a dream' when everything's going well and easily. But have you ever tried to wake yourself up out of a nightmare?"

Laura knew what Nina meant. That feeling of helplessness, of despair and horror as the nightmare monster approached.

Nina continued, "That's the difficult one, isn't it? Sometimes it works – but usually not. We have no control of the dreaming once we're in it."

It was beginning to make sense to Laura. She turned back to the bottles.

Nina sighed. "At least we know that we've got the link to Quin and Randall safe. We're through the most difficult part of it."

"Isn't there anyone else who can help?"

"Haven't you understood any of this? Hiding in the dreaming was a last-ditch measure. Something desperate, last minute. It was that or death! There was no time for anyone else to learn what to do. It was a panic measure!" She stopped suddenly. "Oh, what's the use? Only Wincy and Quinland and Philomena can do it, possibly Randall... There's no one else."

"Can't *you* remember what to do? You must have seen Quinland release water-witches dozens of times?"

"Not that often. You've probably been around almost as many as I have. Did you know what Quin was doing?"

"Not a clue. How about you?"

For a moment they stared at each other. "We could try, I suppose," said Laura at last. "Make it up, I mean."

So they found a china bowl and cleaned it out, and put it amidst some of the fabrics and bedding Randall had taken from Wincy's house.

Very carefully, her hand only slightly trembling, Nina poured the contents of one of the bottles into the bowl.

For a moment they stood there, looking at the tiny bowl of transparent liquid, glinting slightly in the candlelight.

"Go on, then," said Laura.

"No, you do it."

Laura sat down cross-legged on the cushions. She cleared her throat. She remembered how Quinland had always sounded soft and quiet, like rain pattering on a roof. But she didn't know what the words were, or what to say. She tried to remember what it was like to dream, to let the mind go. A kind of relaxation, perhaps. She remembered those faces caught in bottles in a room back at home, she remembered the sound of Wincy's voice and her mother's hands, and Max's smile and these powerful images moved through her mind, carrying it along into another realm...

And then it happened. A shape dimly flickered in the air in front of her and at once disappeared.

Nina said, "There! I saw something!"

"So did I!" The excitement of this was overwhelming. Laura sat still, concentrating once more.

But her excitement got in the way every time. She couldn't let herself drift. She knew what was going wrong. In a way, she was trying too hard.

In the end, tired and stiff, she stood up. "This is ridiculous. Even Randall finds it hard. I'm not getting anywhere now," she said. "Why don't you have a go?"

But Nina was no better. Half-heartedly, she tried to say a few words of welcome, something reassuring, but it sounded out-of-place, absurd.

Without another word they carefully poured the liquid back into the bottle and replaced the stopper.

Max was stirring. They heard mumbled words, half comprehensible, as he tossed and turned. "He's very hot," said Nina, looking worried again.

"Shall I go back to the apothecary?" Laura offered, although she was so weary that she thought she might fall asleep at any moment.

"No. I've got a better idea." Nina was wiping a cool flannel dipped in water over Max's face. He seemed slightly more at ease. "I think you should go and find Ross or Lally. They might have some clues about all this."

"I don't know where they live," Laura said dully. She was more depressed by her failure than she could ever remember. So near and yet so far!

"Randall took you by where Lally lived yesterday, didn't he?"

Down by the river, Laura remembered with difficulty. It seemed like a hundred years ago. That woman who'd been sewing, waiting for her daughter. She supposed she could find them again, so long as she stayed by the left bank of the river.

"If they're not there, where else shall I try?"

"Come back here," Nina said. "I can find Ross quicker than you."

Laura felt a little better. At least she wasn't going to be made to tramp the streets of Bricus endlessly. The river wasn't far away.

"I'll be as quick as I can," she said. "Is there anything else you need for Max?"

"All I need for Max is Quinland, or Wincy, or someone I can trust!"

Laura put her arm round Nina's thin shoulders. For a moment the two girls clung together. Then Laura put on her cloak again and left Silver Street.

She was just in time. It was more difficult than she expected to find exactly the right shack amongst so many poor dwelling-places. But eventually she found one that looked right and as she hesitated, the door opened. Lally came out, arm in arm with her mother. Both of them carried large carpet-bags, as if they were at the start of a journey. They looked up as Laura approached.

"Hello, do you remember me?" Laura asked Lally.

"Yes." The girl's brief reply was noncommittal.

"Nina sent me. We need help."

"What's wrong?" The older woman, with quick warmth, put down her bag. "You look exhausted, girl. What's been happening?"

"It's Randall and Quinland! They're lost in the dreaming. We were attacked by a firefly. There was one hidden in one of the bottles, and Randall and Quinland had to escape quickly. They're in the dreaming, and we don't know how to get them back. We were hoping you might have some idea. And Max was burned by the firefly, and he's not well, he's shaking, and so hot, and we need help!"

"I should say you do." For a moment the mother and daughter looked at each other.

Do you trust her? their looks said. Is she one of us?

Then the older woman shrugged briefly. "I can't reach an aquemancer in the dreaming myself and neither can Lally... but we may be able to help you. You'd better come with us."

"Is it far?" She felt, she absolutely knew, that she couldn't go another step.

"Only a little way. Here, oh, my dear!"

Laura felt herself enfolded in a warm and welcoming hug and her tears soaked into Lally's mother's cloak. She felt a light touch, a soothing stroking of her hair that almost lulled her into calmness.

"I'm sorry," she said at last. "It's not very helpful, is it?"

She saw Lally grin, a quick sympathy that defused her embarrassment. Without any further fuss, Lally and her mother picked up their carpet bags once more and set off at an easy pace and it was possible to keep up with them.

183

"Where are we going?" Laura asked, as they turned away from the river.

"Something happened last night. Both Lally and I saw Wincy in our dreams. She showed us a way through. There's a place of significance which the Pyromancer hasn't found yet. We may be able to contact her there. It's only a chance, but worth a try. You caught us just in time."

"You saw Wincy? In your dreams? Really?"

"Yes. Hey, what is it? What's the matter?"

She couldn't believe it. After all this. They were going to find Wincy.

Another long tramp through the city, through areas she did not recognize at all. They talked all the time.

"Has she appeared in dreams before?" Laura asked right away. "Randall and Quinland have been going mad looking for her."

"Only last night." Mother and daughter glanced at each other. "Last night, Wincy told us where she and the Lady Philomena and her father can be found. They had to lie low for ages in case the Pyromancer was using spies. But it's got too urgent now. The Pyromancer has found out how to use aquemancy and is sending fireflies through to the dreaming. We were going to tell Quin, if Wincy hadn't managed to get through. Perhaps we still can."

They were passing quietly by grand old houses, their balconies and windows shining in the twilight. They heard the sound of music and dancing and chattering. There were quiet gardens set in the centre of elegant squares, gardens where the fountains had been turned off. The leaves on the trees were dusty, tinged with brown, as if autumn were not far away.

"I hate this hot weather," muttered Lally to her mother. "When's it all going to come right, when can we stop hiding away like this?"

"Not long, I hope. Now that we've got every hope of getting Wincy and the Countess back with us again, and the others, soon we'll do it. We'll be prepared this time. The Pyromancer won't have a chance against all of us!"

It was a comforting thought, Laura thought, but they hadn't yet contacted Wincy, and Randall and Quinland were still locked away in their watery enchantments.

It was tiredness that made her so depressed. It had been the most traumatic day of her life.

At last they turned down a narrow alley between two blocks of apartments. "Not far now," said Lally to Laura, and then Lally's mother suddenly thrust out her arm, holding them back.

"Shhhh," she whispered. "Something's wrong…"

They saw that the alley opened out into a wide square. A crowd of people stood there, many of them in uniform. Beyond them, a vast cage contained a firefly. Laura could see the fizzes and sparks flying through the air above the crowd.

Marguerite, Lally's mother, said, "Oh no, not this…"

She seemed to pull herself together. "Come on girls, we're too late. Let's get out of this –"

She turned, as if to shepherd the two girls back to the main street.

But Laura had seen someone. Had seen, beneath the gaudy uniform, a figure step into the light from a doorway, a figure she recognized, a set to the shoulders and head she knew better than her own.

"Darius!" she cried, tearing herself away from Lally and her mother. Not this time. She wasn't going to let him go this time. She rushed down the alley towards the soldiers.

"Darius!" she shouted once more and the soldier with his back to her swung round.

His visor showed nothing, but he brought up his sword aggressively, as if to ward her off.

"It's me! Laura!"

"Get out of here! If you know what's good for you."

And it *was* Darius, her own brother's voice, coldly dismissing her as if she were a stranger.

"Darius, stop it! This isn't a game, please –"

But the soldier had turned away from her and she found herself staring into the visor of another man, a tall figure in cloth-of-gold, a visored mask completely concealing his features.

She took a step backwards. It was too late. His gauntleted hand reached out and seized her wrist. "Darius Alderwood Brooke," said a sibilant voice.

Her brother snapped smartly to attention.

"This girl seems to know you. Who is she?"

And then at last Darius raised the visor to his helmet and Laura saw his familiar features staring at her with complete indifference.

She wanted to wail, to scream and shout at him, but something held her back, and it wasn't just the Pyromancer's grip.

Something had happened to Darius's eyes. Something gleamed behind his eyes, green like her own, something that shone, golden as fire, cloudy as smoke.

It looked as if his brain were on fire and his eyes nothing more than windows through to a furnace.

"I knew her before," said her brother and his voice was passionless and empty.

"Her name?" the Pyromancer asked.

"Laura Alderwood Brooke."

"Your *sister*?"

"My twin." And then Darius lowered the visor to his helmet and turned his back on them.

The Pyromancer's grip on her arm tightened.

"Watch this, then," he hissed in her ear. "Watch

what becomes of meddlesome water-witches. Report back to your friends. Tell them what you have seen here. Tell them how powerful I am, that aquemancy is merely a tool for me."

Half fainting, Laura saw the soldiers make a wide space in the centre of the square round an intricately wrought fountain. Unlike every other fountain in Bricus, this one still flowed. In the sudden silence, Laura could hear the water splashing, cascading from two intertwined bronze dolphins.

The Pyromancer released her and walked slowly towards the fountain, almost as if reluctant to approach the silvery water. His right hand rose up to shoulder height, the fingers spread wide over the dolphin fountain.

He was about to speak. Laura wanted to interrupt, to cause a diversion, anything, to stop the Pyromancer using the skills of aquemancy. She knew what was going to happen.

Words, softly uttered below the level of conscious hearing. The gentle spashing of water ceased. Somewhere to the side of the fountain, a cloud flickered and faded through indeterminate shapes. The Pyromancer's voice repeated the words, and the cloud slowly solidified.

And then Laura found herself blinking and missed the moment of manifestation. There, by the edge of the fountain, an elderly man dressed in velvet and lace stared around in some be-wilderment. A murmur ran through the crowd, as the Pyromancer gave a quick order. At once several soldiers stepped forward and seized the old man.

"Oh stop, stop!" Laura couldn't bear it. The old man looked so helpless, so alone. He staggered slightly, stumbling against the fountain. And then she saw Darius move forward, to join the other soldiers.

She saw him haul the old man away from the water and clip handcuffs round his wrists. There was blood running from the side of the old man's mouth. A couple of words from her brother, an order she couldn't hear and the old man was marched away through one of the backstreets.

Silence for a moment, and then the Pyromancer raised his right arm once more. Chilled, although the night was hot and stuffy, Laura recognized the same pattern of syllables.

She was gripped by apprehension. Who else would the Pyromancer conjure forth? Wincy? The Countess? Who else was still hiding, waiting in the dreaming?

Marguerite and Lally had joined her on the edge of the square. They were clinging together. "Can't you do anything?" Laura whispered to them frantically. "Please, can't you even *try*?"

"Against *that*?" Marguerite's face was haunted.

"The firefly would kill us all in minutes if we attempted anything. There's no chance."

Laura couldn't help herself. She couldn't give up like that. She began to move away from them, round the edges of the square. She kept to the shadow of doorways, taking care not to make a sound. All the time, another of those frail clouds flickered, gradually coalescing into solidity. And again Laura missed the actual moment of manifestation. She wondered afterwards if anyone ever saw what really happened, whether any observer always blinked or looked away at the crucial moment. Perhaps it was part of the magic.

A beautiful woman, frail and delicate in wafting green silk, stood there by the fountain. With fury she turned on the Pyromancer, her hands spread towards him like weapons.

The Pyromancer's gauntleted hand chopped through the air. And at once the firefly was released from its cage, tearing into the square with a rush of heat and flame.

The soldiers didn't move. Had they been trained not to flinch, Laura wondered? But the firefly went no further. It maintained a distance from the beautiful woman and Laura saw her hands fall, her shoulders slump as if she had lost everything.

And then she realized she could hear what the Pyromancer was saying. His voice was little more than a whisper, but the words seemed amplified by the hissing in his tone. "Come, Countess. The game's over. I can use the dreaming too. Every last trick is mine."

"Because you cheat!" she said bitterly.

"Because I am the stronger. There was no need to cheat."

"You spread lies! You are the Liar Serpent –"

"Silence! Do you want your lady-in-waiting to become food for my firefly?" He bent his visored face towards her. "Go quietly with my men or watch your precious Wincy burn."

Laura saw the Countess allow the soldiers to manacle her wrists together. She was marched away after the old man, and for a moment Laura thought that the Pyromancer would follow her.

But instead he gave one more signal to the firefly, which sent out a tremendous burst of flame towards the stone base of the dolphin fountain. Immediately the water began to bubble and boil and in less than a minute, every last drop had evaporated.

The Pyromancer compelled the firefly back into the cage with a few brief words Laura could not understand. The door clanged shut. On its cart, the cage was carried over the cobbles and away from the square. Laura slumped against the wall, miserable tears in her eyes. She had missed none of the significance of what had happened. The water in the fountain had been their last chance of getting Wincy back.

She would be lost, marooned in the dreaming for ever. There was no way to reach her now, not ever again.

Leaning against the warm stone wall, Laura felt water running down her face.

But it wasn't tears.

Rain.

CHAPTER 17

Rainfall

She didn't think she'd sleep, but somehow she managed it. Lally and Marguerite had found her, wandering dazed some way from the square, and had taken her back to Silver Street where they tried to explain everything to Max and Nina.

The Countess and her father, captured. Wincy, lost for ever. Visions of fireflies and the dolphin fountain haunted them all. Their hope of releasing Randall or Quinland from the dreaming was more remote than ever.

Max was sitting up, looking rather better. Marguerite found some salve in her carpet bag which seemed to draw the pain from his burns. And thanks to the apothecary's potions and ointments, there was no infection.

He moved over on the cushions to let Laura sit down and that was the last she knew of anything that day.

She dreamed of people without heads, with plumes of fire and smoke rising from their shoulders. She tried to run away from the fire people but they turned into dragons with scaly skin, soaring through the air, blowing vicious flames at her, and she had nowhere to go, no possible means of escape.

Except there was someone shouting her name, calling to her. Someone had her by the hand, pulling her away from the fire-dragons, taking her somewhere safe...

It was Wincy who was calling.

Wincy, in the dreaming.

Her hair was loose, flowing over her shoulders like water. She was dressed in grey, a filmy, floaty fabric shot through with blues and greens. From the ends of her fingers, from the strands of her hair, from the drifting hems of her robe, water fell. Lightly and softly, it splashed around her like rain and at first Laura thought that Wincy must be crying, that this water was her way of weeping.

But her cousin's face was smiling, her eyes creased with amusement.

"Come, Laura," she said. "There is no time for unhappiness now. You have work to do."

"But Wincy, how can we get you back? Tell me how to do it!"

She shook her head. "Never mind that now. There's something urgent for you to do, if we're ever to save Bricus from the Pyromancer. Listen carefully to me."

Laura put out her hand to touch Wincy's fingers and all she could feel was water, running softly over her skin. "Wincy, is this *really* you? Or am I just dreaming?"

"You're dreaming, Laura, but dreams are important. There's no 'just' about it. Now, pay attention." She told Laura what to do, and it was the scariest thing she had ever heard, more risky and dangerous than anything that had happened so far.

At the end of it, Wincy said, "I know you can do this, Laura. I've been watching you all these years. Your mother kept me up to date. It's why I sent you all those bottles. I knew you would find significances in them one day, you were always so sensitive to the influences, like Cytheria... You could become an aquemancer too, if you work hard..."

"Oh, will you teach me?"

"You'll have to find someone else, Laura." There was sadness in her tone and she stepped backwards, away from Laura. She seemed dimmer, more indistinct. Laura tried to reach her, stretching out her arms to hold her back, but Wincy was fading from her, returning to the mysterious dreaming where water fell from her fingers.

Laura began to cry, and it was Max who woke her up, his right hand on hers, softly calling her name.

She was confused at first. In the dim light of the one candle she almost didn't recognize who he was. His face, red and shiny on one side, looked as if he was wearing a harlequin mask and for a moment she wondered if she was still in the dream, returning to the nightmare world where Wincy had found her.

"Laura! Stop it! Come on, you've been dreaming. Laura, wake up!"

"Oh…" She covered her face with her hands. She felt impossibly distressed, but she didn't know why. She could remember nothing of her dream. The everyday reality of Max, with his burned face and kind voice, pushed every memory from her mind. Except that of Darius, looking at her as if he'd never known her. "I – oh, Max, what am I going to do? Darius didn't know me, there's something horribly wrong with him, he's been taken over."

"I know." He looked grim. "Marguerite told me. I don't think there's much we can do about it right now. We need Quin or Randall or Wincy, they'd be able to help."

"But they're all trapped!" There was something there in the back of her mind but she couldn't reach it... "They're no use to us now. Ever since I got here we've been waiting for someone else to solve things. We've been waiting for Wincy or Randall and Quin to defeat the Pyromancer, but it was never any use. And Randall didn't want me to do anything, he didn't want me to know anything. He wanted to keep me powerless –"

"He was trying to protect you."

"I know! But what use is that, now? We can't do anything on our own, we have to wait for them to get us out of this mess, and what use are they? Where are they?"

She felt his good arm over her shoulder, and it was a relief to lean against him. On the other side of the room, Nina was fast asleep in one of the chairs. Lally and Marguerite had gone.

"What do you know, Max? Wincy took you and Nina in, you've been working with Randall and Quinland all this time. How much aquemancy do you *know*?"

For a moment he didn't move. Then he stood up, slowly and carefully, and held his hand out to her. In silence he led her across the floor to the stairs and she went up them first, holding the trapdoor open for him.

The noise was louder here. It had been going on all night, although she hadn't really registered what it was, far beneath the ground. That softest of pattering, complicated and constant, the falling of water on the garden shed, on the garden outside, all over the city of Bricus.

Rain. Max and Laura stood in the door to the shed, watching it darken the soil, beating down the heads of the chrysanthemums with gentle pressure, shining over the stones of the path. The coolness of the night air was like balm.

"We swim in water in the womb, before we're born," said Max quietly. "Our bodies are composed of eighty per cent water. Our blood is nearly all water. It's not so very strange, really, that some of us can transform...

"Some of us live in it." He turned towards her. "You know about the arethusans, don't you? Some people call them mermaids, some think that they're a strange mix, somewhere between a human and a seal and a dolphin. They're actually closer to humans than anything else, but they prefer to stay in water. They are the source of magic in our world, and some of us share their power. Wincy and Randall, for example, have arethusan blood somewhere in their history. So do you, because you'd never have been able to pick out those bottles with such sure skill otherwise. The Alderwood family must have intermarried with an arethusan at some stage. As did my and Nina's grandfather. In fact, most of the water-witches you've met here have some connection with arethusans.

"The Countess is part arethusan, through her father's side. Lord Dulchimer has been powerful in his time, but he's old now and no longer influential. It meant so much that the Earl should have married his daughter, one of us! We thought that at last we would have some kind of status, instead of always being regarded at best as fairground acts and at worst as evil enchanters. But at the time Marrin seemed to be genuinely sympathetic to the arethusans. He even made some effort to learn aquemancy, I remember Quinland saying. But it all changed when Lerris arrived and we're under attack now, and I don't know who we can ask. Wherever we go, whatever we do, the Earl's men will be watching for us, they and their horrible fireflies."

"Max." Her voice was low. "Where do the fireflies come from? How are they made? What are they?"

In her mind, fresh from the nightmare, she saw her brother's face, with flames in his eyes. Was he being changed, was he actually *becoming* a firefly?

"I've heard that they were invented by scientists in Rustria. Or that they were discovered under the Southern Mountains. But the Rustrians used them first, as a kind of sentient weapon, something created only to destroy. And they are fuelled by animal life. They reproduce only after killing a human. They seem to absorb the essence of the creature they kill. What's the matter, Laura?"

And so she told him what she'd seen in Darius's eyes.

"I've never heard of such a thing," he said slowly. "But it must be some kind of fire-based enchantment, something that's taken your brother from you. And if it happened one way, there's no reason to think that it can't be reversed."

He was trying to cheer her up. "How, though? How would we even begin?"

"Just a moment. I think we're missing out something here." He looked up briefly into the sky. The rain seemed to have set in for the night. It was sheeting across the garden in great washes of water. It was very dark, no sign of moon or stars between racing clouds.

A wind was blowing up. Lightning then, briefly flashing over the city, throwing into relief the pale and ghostly shapes of flowers and trees and houses. In that instant of illumination, Laura looked at Max's face.

His eyes were wide, thoughtfully scanning the skies.

"This storm," she said. "Are there often storms at midsummer in Bricus?"

"No." A lift in his voice, something upbeat and positive. "No, there are never storms in summer.

This is something else. Someone's made this happen –" The crack of thunder drowned his next words.

And suddenly it all fell into place. She remembered her dream, every last detail of it. She remembered what Wincy had told her to do.

"Max!" she said. "I know what must be done! Wincy told me, while I was dreaming! Listen to this."

She told him every step of the plan, and he shook his head, incredulously. "It's madness. Lunatic. You can't possibly—"

"Wincy said so! And it makes sense, you know it does!"

He stared at her, frowning. "No. It's far too dangerous. We'll have to get the other aquemancers together and consult them—"

"It will take too long!"

"I can't let you do this. Not on your own." He looked implacable, and she knew she would have to argue it to the bitter end.

"Wincy told me to," she said stubbornly. "It's Wincy's plan and anyway what's the alternative? Have you any other ideas?"

Slowly, he shook his head. "All right. It's as good a time as any, I suppose. Fireflies can't bear water. They won't be out tonight, while it's raining. I suppose this might even be our best chance."

There was a flash of lightning again and she saw that he was considering her doubtfully. His words were nearly lost in a deep rumble of thunder.

She persuaded him to return to the hideout for warm clothes, and to take another dose of the potion Marguerite had left. He looked so much better that she was greatly encouraged. They woke up Nina and told her what they were going to do. Laura insisted that she should know what was happening. "We're in this mess because people didn't communicate. We can't make the same mistake."

"But can't I come too?" Nina asked. She was still half asleep, her hair tousled. She yawned.

"No, you stay here. There's no point in all of us getting into danger. There ought to be someone here anyway, to tell the others if –"

"If it doesn't work?" Nina looked anxious.

"We'll be careful," said Max. He gave her a brief hug. "Look after yourself, sis. We'll be back soon."

It was still raining, although the sky was lightening in the east. A slow, dull dawn, cast over by heavy skies and the unseasonal wind.

They made for the palace, down past the shacks where Marguerite and Lally lived. Max paused there for a moment outside their door.

"Shall we wake them up? Tell them what we're doing?" asked Laura, realizing.

He nodded. They tried the door but there was

no reply. Laura tried the handle and it swung open. The room inside was chaos. It had been ransacked. Every drawer was open, every chair tumbled. Max said, "I hope they got out. I hope they weren't still here…"

"Was it the Pyromancer?" she asked.

He nodded. "He must have found out where they've been hiding. He's getting more powerful. I just hope they got away in time."

He was standing at one of the windows, as if he was on the lookout. But as she watched, he leaned forward and breathed out on the cold window pane.

His breath misted over the glass. Except there was something written there, a message cutting through the condensation of his breath.

It was gone before she could see it. He wiped his hand over the glass, so that no one else would be able to revive the few, simple words.

"I know where they are." He smiled at her again and she saw at once how relieved he was. "They've left Bricus. They've gone out into the country to drum up support. They'll be safe, but no use to us right now."

"We'll manage," she said, although she could hardly bear to contemplate what she had to do.

"You're not an aquemancer, Laura," he said. "Are you sure about this?"

"Yes," she said quietly. "I tried to release

Randall or Quin from one of those bottles, and it nearly worked. There was a shadowy figure … but I couldn't concentrate in the right way, I didn't know how."

"All aquemancers need teaching," he said. "But I suppose it's a start."

They left the shack and were walking alongside the river, while the rain bucketed down on them. Beneath the sheeting water, she saw him regarding her again. Their eyes met for a moment and then he looked away.

He was not as obviously handsome as Randall; indeed there was something slightly lopsided about his eyebrows, slightly off centre about the way his mouth curled when he was amused.

He was not much taller than she, not much older. She had only known him for a few days but it felt like a lifetime. He was never pompous like the other men in her life. He treated her like an equal. She wondered what her father and Darius would make of him, if they ever met. She assumed, somehow, that her mother would like him…

Max became aware of her scrutiny. He raised an eyebrow.

"My mother had webbed fingers," said Laura slowly. "She's always brilliant at forecasting the weather, too."

He picked up her hand and regarded it closely.

"And so have you, Laura. Magic at your fingertips, and no wonder if your own mother is a water-witch."

She felt a shiver of excitement. "What does it mean, magic at your fingertips?"

"Everything. Or nothing." He sounded thoughtful. "It's complicated. Your mother is not the only water-witch to refuse to practise. Aquemancy is viewed with suspicion nearly everywhere in Bricus. It quite often runs only through the female line and that can cause trouble. Some men get very jealous."

She would have liked to discuss this further, but then she realized where they were.

Above them loomed a tall structure of stone, recently decorated with gaudy pictures of dragons and suns. There was a narrow gate set in the base of it, with heavily armed soldiers on either side.

Far away, indistinct under the wash of rain, the glass roofs were running with water.

"I don't like this, Laura." Max stopped. "It's too much of a risk. How do we know that the Pyromancer will do as you want?"

"Of course he will! The Pyromancer won't be able to resist it. Two real live aquemancers to play with, to feed to his horrible fireflies!"

"And then what?" He looked at her steadily. "What if Quin and Randall are killed, like all the others?"

205

"No! Surely they're powerful enough!" She sounded confident, but inwardly she was terrified. "We'll have to chance it, Max. Whatever other hope is there?"

"We could lie low. Wait for the other aquemancers to find the way through to the dreaming –"

"But the Pyromancer is using it already! And anyway, Wincy *told* me to do this! And Darius, my twin brother, is there in the palace and that's important! I wouldn't be there alone, Darius would –"

Darius's eyes, filled with fire. She was shaking again. Max'll stop me, she thought. Like my father and Darius and Randall, he won't let me do this –

But Max stood aside, his face grave. For a moment he rested his hand on her shoulder. And then Laura turned away and went straight up to the main gate of the palace.

CHAPTER 18

Execution

There were no water-witches to attend Franklin. His wounds festered and blistered. His fever raged and ebbed and raged again. Sometimes, at the heights of delirium, he shouted out the names of strangers, but no one ever came.

Only Darius visited Franklin. At the end of the day's duties he climbed the stairs to the wing where the infirmary was and went to sit by his friend's bedside. Darius told Franklin about what had happened that day, what exercises had taken place and how he, Darius, had fared. Sometimes Franklin seemed to be listening but more often his mind was flaring around like so many fireworks and nothing seemed to catch his attention.

Darius bathed his hands and face with cool water, grudgingly given by the attendant, a vague, short-sighted man who looked rather puzzled to see Darius there. Sometimes Franklin could be calmed by the patient drone of Darius's voice. After he had recounted the events of the day, Darius tried to think of other things to tell Franklin, but his own mind was curiously blank.

He started by trying to remember his own past. "We lived in the country," he said, one evening. "Three hundred miles from Bricus to the north, my parents –"

But he could remember nothing definite about them. Had they been farmers? Or shopkeepers? His father he could vaguely recall, a soldier who taught him to throw knives, to pull a bow...

There was a blank where his mother was. Someone kind, he thought, someone who was always there, usually good-humoured... But what did she look like? What was her voice like?

And was he an only child? He had no recollection of any other figure in his childhood. There was really very little to tell Franklin. "I grew up there," he said. "Went to school, did all the usual things. And we had relatives in Bricus and they were always going on about how great it was here, and so we came."

He stopped. *We?* He and who else?

Nothing. Not a whisper, not the faintest remnant of memory. There was no other person in his past, nothing he could tell his friend about.

And so Franklin tossed and turned, and Darius told him boring stories about the day's events, and hardly realized that anything was missing.

He walked back to the Earl's palace where, every night, the Pyromancer presided over the evening meal. Every night, he repeated a blessing over the food and scattered scarlet powder over every dish.

And in the end it was the spice that prevailed. Every night Darius remembered less and less about who he was and where he came from.

And the fire behind his eyes ate further into his brain.

At length, Franklin began to heal. Some days after the encounter with the firefly, about when the rains started, he sat up in bed for the first time and ate a bowl of onion soup. The skin on his hands and arms and over most of his body was puckered and distorted by burns, but miraculously his face was clear. He managed a slight smile as Darius arrived again that evening.

"What, you again? Haven't you anything better to do?"

Darius's hair was plastered flat by the rain, and his clothes were beginning to steam in the heat of the infirmary. He'd brought a bag of apples. He emptied them into a bowl on Franklin's bedside table, and sat down.

"Well, I could always start volume 14 of the Brican Civil Wars. Or make notes on Pender's *Military Tactics*. And there's always the *Life of General Bartolo*."

"So you thought you'd come and tell me more tales of life home on the farm."

"I didn't know whether you were listening."

"It's your voice, Darius. I kept trying to sleep, but there you'd be, droning on…"

Darius grinned at him. He was immensely cheered to find Franklin in such excellent form, although he could see that Franklin was having trouble holding the spoon. "By rights, it should have been me lying there," he said, more solemnly.

"Great lummock. You didn't know what to do." Franklin leaned back against the pillows, pushing the half finished bowl of soup away. He looked very tired.

Darius stood up, wandering round the ward. Franklin was the only occupant. There were no pictures on the walls, nothing to relieve the stark efficiency of the place. Just the usual sunburst design carved in the wood of the door. The attendant was in his office further down the corridor. It was very quiet, although in the distance, Darius was aware of the rain pounding away.

"How much longer have you got here?" he asked. "When will they let you out?"

"I don't know, they don't tell me anything." Franklin's eyes were closed. Darius wondered if he was drifting off again. He began to tiptoe to the door.

"Darius." Franklin's voice was very quiet.

He stopped, looking back. His friend's face was turned away from him.

"Darius, what about Laura? Have you heard anything?"

Darius stared at him. "Who?"

"Laura. You remember, you told me all about her. You sent me to find her –" He stopped. "And Wincy, someone else –"

Darius frowned, trying to remember. Perhaps the names were familiar ... people he went to school with? But even as he tried to pin the memory down it seemed to dissipate and vanish. He shrugged. "Sorry, I think you must have been dreaming. I don't know anyone called Laura or Wincy." He was merely puzzled now, not in the least worried or anxious.

Franklin's head turned on the pillow. He watched Darius cross the room. "What's that on your hand?" he asked, as Darius reached the door.

Darius glanced down at his palm. The mark of the dragon had developed a strange scaly appearance. It no longer hurt.

He said, "Just … a tattoo. It's nothing much. See you soon, Franklin."

Franklin found it difficult to sleep that night.

The awful thing was that Darius had no idea that there was anything wrong. He was kept so active, physically and mentally, so busy with all the exercises, the drills, the volumes of military history, that he didn't even realize that his memory of the past was full of the most surprising holes.

He had seen very little of Perrian since they had been on guard duty together. He was rather startled to find Perrian coming up to meet him on his way down from the infirmary.

"Been to visit your friend in the ranks again?" he said nastily. "Got quite a taste for low life, haven't you?"

"He saved my life!" Darius was shocked.

"He tried to kill a firefly."

"It was attacking!"

"Fortunately, he didn't succeed," Perrian continued.

"What? What do you mean, he didn't succeed? I saw it collapse into a sticky black mess –"

"A firefly can be revived from that state, as well you know. Though no thanks to Franklin Laclos, it's proved difficult… Anyway, I didn't come to talk about your slummy friends. You'll have a chance to see what's become of that firefly tomorrow. There's going to be an execution."

"An execution?" Darius knew he sounded stupid but he was taken aback by the unfriendliness of Perrian's attitude.

"Yes," said Perrian. They were walking around the quad beneath the cloisters. The rain still fell, and the quad itself was a sea of mud. "Two executions, actually. The Countess Philomena and her father are going to meet several fireflies tomorrow. That'll warm them up." He scowled at the dark clouds racing over the quad. "Could do with it, a bit of warmth, don't you think? Anyway, it should prove ... interesting."

"*Why?* Was there a trial? Have I missed something?"

But Darius knew that there had been no trial. It would have been news all over the city, the trial of the Earl's wife...

"She's a water-witch, of course," said Perrian. "And she's been unfaithful to the Earl. You've heard all this already, don't be a fool." He shrugged. "It was only a matter of time before they'd finally cop it. What business has a water-witch interfering in the affairs of Bricus? Good riddance, I say." He looked down his nose at Darius. "The Pyromancer wants all the new recruits on duty, so brace yourself. It's going to be hot work."

He laughed unpleasantly and brushed past Darius as if they had never been friends.

Executions took place in the main square outside the palace. Everyone knew that. So Darius was puzzled to discover that these two executions were to take place in the Pyromancer's own quarters in the palace, far away from the public rooms and the Earl's own apartments.

"It's raining," explained Jasper as they lined up ready outside the door. "We can't risk the fireflies getting wet." His voice was steady as ever and no one could see his eyes behind the visor. But Darius saw that his hand was clenched rather too firmly on the hilt of his sword, and wondered if Jasper were nervous.

He was still speaking. "I must remind you to do nothing – *nothing* – without permission. Don't move a finger, don't twitch or sigh or even blink. There will be fireflies there, more than you've ever seen before. One move out of order and you're fried. The Pyromancer lives amongst the fireflies and can control them. But they're jumpy, nervous... You'll need to be careful." He paused. "They're also very curious. You'll see. Now, are you ready?"

They all saluted.

Jasper opened the door.

*　　*　　*

It was a greenhouse. A vast hallway made of glass, sweltering hot, a dry heat that rasped in the throat, although the sky overhead was still black with thunderclouds and the rain still drenched the surface of the glass. The heat came from a large fireplace set in the one marble wall on the south side of the room and from a number of torches held in freestanding candelabra. The vaulted roof rose in peaks and turrets over them, and everywhere over their heads, the ceiling was straddled by narrow beams of shining silvery metal.

Later, Darius noticed that there was very little furniture, nothing conventionally comfortable about the room. No carpets, no easy chairs. One or two benches, a table, and the heavy wrought iron candelabra, taller than a man, that was all. The candlelight did something to dispel the gloom but not much. It didn't matter.

Darius paid no attention to the furniture because up above them, swooping between the silvery beams like monstrous birds, were the fireflies.

They screamed as they darted through the darkened air, high-pitched wails that set the teeth on edge. As the terrified squadron of conscripts stood there, hardly daring to breathe, they swooped lower and lower towards them and Darius saw their evil red eyes glinting, felt the searing heat of their breath on his hands.

He kept still. He neither flinched nor blinked as

the sickly, wafting stink of sulphur hit his face. It took every ounce of control.

He was fascinated. He had never seen anything so beautiful, so utterly terrifying. They moved so quickly, faster than he had ever imagined possible! The crippled firefly he had seen in that back kitchen in Bricus bore no resemblance to these extraordinary creatures, circling through the burning air. They were magnificent, powerful, appallingly dangerous.

The Pyromancer stood slightly to one side by the fire, and the light from the flames caught on the gold of his helmet and cloth so that he seemed to shine like a god. He stood there as if he needed the warmth, although the room was unthinkably hot as it was.

What would it be like when the rain stopped, Darius thought? When the sun shone through those faceted panes of glass? Who could possibly bear it then? Perrian had marched across the room to stand at the Pyromancer's side. Darius felt jealous. Why should Perrian be so honoured? And then he remembered his dream, the way Perrian had lifted the Pyromancer's helmet.

They were related. All that stuff about Jasper being Perrian's father was no more than a bluff. Perrian and the Pyromancer shared the same dry quality in their voices, the same set of the shoulders.

Darius was entranced, bemused, astounded by everything the Pyromancer did and said. He found the Pyromancer's voice compelling, he had no desire ever to disobey. His envy for Perrian dissipated, leaving only respect, that he should be so close to this god-like being...

And yet, when he saw the prisoners brought in through a side door and lined up in front of the Pyromancer, ready to receive the kiss of the firefly, something in him revolted.

He recognized them, of course. He had been present when the Pyromancer had enticed the Countess and her father from the dreaming. But what harm could they do anyone now? They were heavily laden with chains, and the woman's hair was dishevelled. The two prisoners stood there calmly, with utmost dignity, while the fire-flies' screams swirled and skittered into the stratosphere.

Although he remembered who they were, his memory was full of gaps. He had no idea that he had promised the Countess his loyalty, that he had shaken hands with the man. But still he could not take his eyes off the woman. She was beautiful, with her silvery-blonde hair and delicate build. He'd seen a portrait of her in the Earl's chambers. Would it be destroyed now? Hung in some attic, out of the way?

It struck him as rather sad. And yet he still

wondered, briefly, if perhaps he'd met her before somewhere else. Long ago, perhaps?

The man was dressed in stained and torn velvet and an old-fashioned cravat. He looked frail but his head was held high.

Neither prisoner looked up to the rafters. They showed no sign at all of noticing the fireflies.

And then Jasper gave instructions for the Guard to separate into pairs, to stand by each of the doors, as if the prisoners might make some mad dash to escape, although the chains they were wearing looked heavy enough to weigh down a carthorse.

Darius was stationed by the door to the Earl's quarters, at some distance from the prisoners.

At first the Pyromancer ignored the prisoners. He was still concentrating on the fireflies, his helmeted head tracking their dizzy movements.

Darius stood to attention by the big double doors and looked up. He was so fascinated by the action of the fireflies that he did not at first realize that the door behind him was slowly opening.

The Pyromancer had raised his hands towards the fireflies, as if calling them down to the ground, and their cries grew to ear-splitting intensity. He began to cross the floor towards the two captives, and the fireflies' circling movements came closer to the ground.

He stopped in front of the woman, and made as if to touch her face, but something in the slant of his helmet made Darius think that the Pyromancer was looking at him...

Or at the door, standing open behind him.

Darius didn't dare look round. He knew it was all right, because none of the soldiers stationed at the exits opposite him were doing anything other than stand to attention...

He stood to attention too, aware that someone important had just entered. And it was the Earl himself who brushed past him and Darius saw that the Pyromancer was taken aback.

The Earl spoke immediately. "There's a girl at the gate. She has two glass phials with her and claims that they contain the link through to two powerful aquemancers." His voice was strangely expressionless. All the time, his eyes looked only at the Pyromancer.

His cold voice continued, very quietly. "I think you might be wise to examine these phials before carrying through this ceremony."

"Is this a delaying tactic, my Lord?"

Even Darius was rather shocked by this. It seemed that the Pyromancer was openly challenging the Earl.

Marrin hesitated. For a moment, no more, his eyes met those of his wife. Was there a message there? A memory of something else? When he spoke, Marrin's voice was still soft. "Lerris, I think you should see this girl first."

A silence, lasting too long. Was the Pyromancer going to argue? Then he inclined his helmeted head slightly and the Earl turned to face Darius.

"Get the girl from the gatehouse," he ordered.

Darius saluted and turned on his heel.

Laura saw her brother coming towards her and it was all she could do not to call out to him, not to run and grab hold of him.

Instead, tall and unfamiliar in his ridiculous helmet and silly, garishly-coloured uniform, he motioned for her to precede him back along the corridor.

She wanted to turn and shout at him. To say, how can you, Darius? How can you forget who you are, what I am? What's happened to you, why have you changed so much?

But instead Laura walked calmly down the endless corridor, knowing that at the end, where the bronze double doors stood, the Pyromancer waited.

She no longer held the glass phials. She was not sure where they were, but she had to believe that the soldier who'd taken them from her as soon as she'd arrived would have them safe somewhere.

The plan wouldn't work otherwise. She needed to be in the same room, under the same roof, as the phials for the plan to have any hope of success.

Laura stood still when she came to the doors, and Darius reached round her to push them open. She could smell him, slightly sweaty, so familiar, so dear.

"Darry," she whispered. "Come on, think, it's *me*!"

But the helmeted head gave no sign even of hearing, let alone understanding.

He pushed her into the huge room and the first person she saw was the Countess Philomena, shackled in chains.

"My Lady!" she cried, without thinking. "What are you – ?" And then she stopped, knowing that this wasn't any use at all.

And became aware of the fireflies, darting around overhead, the stink of sulphur and the enormous heat from the fire by the wall.

"You know the Countess?" The man in the sunburst helmet with the elaborate regalia was hissing at her like a snake. "Oh yessss…" he mused. "The street urchin at the scene of arrest. You witnessed it all, didn't you, Laura Alderwood?"

Laura could say nothing, do nothing. She saw, with a sudden intake of breath, that another soldier had approached the Pyromancer with a tray on which stood the glass phials.

And all the time her eyes were drawn upwards, up to the creatures wildly flinging themselves through the darkened air as if they were escaping from the pits of hell itself.

"Now what have we here?" murmured the Pyromancer. He picked up one of the phials and squinted at one of the burning torches through it.

Then he unscrewed the stopper and smelled the contents. A few drops were allowed to fall on the wrist of his gauntlet and he examined them closely, twisting his hand this way and that.

"Where did you get these, girl?" he shot at her.

"Sir, an aquemancer of my acquaintance, one Ross, gave them to me. He told me to keep them safe, that he would process the contents when the present danger was over..."

"And what possessed you to bring them here?"

She had been well prepared for these questions. She hung her head and spoke quietly. Too quietly.

"What's that? Speak up, girl!"

The Pyromancer had come closer.

"I didn't believe him, sir. I didn't think he could do it."

"And you knew I could?" Something glinted behind the visor of the Pyromancer's helmet. "Such an old trick," he commented. "Just like the ogre who was made to transform himself into a mouse... So, what we have here are the links to a couple of powerful aquemancers, capable, you and your friends think, of outwitting me..."

He laughed, quite the most revolting sound Laura had ever heard.

"Can't you, then?"

The Earl had had enough. He strode across the floor to the Pyromancer and quite deliberately smashed his hand across the tray.

The phials fell to the floor and shattered against the stone. A small quantity of transparent liquid splashed across the marble.

No screaming, no terrible cries of anguish. Merely a feeling of coldness, of energy draining away. Even the Pyromancer seemed to feel it. He hesitated, as if unsure.

In that pause, that brief hesitation, Laura tried to catch the Countess's attention. She moved her hand, very slightly, so that the lapel of her jacket fell open.

Two bottles glinted there, plain, unadorned, clear glass. They were unstoppered.

"The Countess can do it," Ross had said. "Just let her see the phial."

It had seemed reasonable enough. But now, with the Pyromancer and the Earl and surrounded by soldiers, how could the Countess begin to concentrate?

She would be stopped. It had to be done quietly, out of sight...

Laura had no time to think. She could only act. She said to the Pyromancer, "It doesn't matter.

There are dozens of us now, we managed to find nearly all the lost witches and they're all ready for you – "

The Pyromancer strode up to her and grabbed her hand. He whirled her round so that her back was to him and forced her hand out towards the Earl.

"See?" came the vile hissing sound in her ear. "See? She's one of them, look between the third and fourth fingers."

Reluctantly, it seemed, Marrin approached her and glanced at her hand. He was rather pale, his skin waxy with sweat. He said, "Let her be, Lerris. Isn't this enough?"

Then he turned away and looked directly at Philomena, his wife.

She raised her chin. "What's this, Marrin? Remnants of a conscience reasserting itself?"

"Shut up!" There was huge violence in his voice. He waved his hand at Laura. "Chain her up!"

Laura didn't struggle. This was what she wanted, and besides, if she moved too abruptly she might spill something from the bottles in her inner pocket.

At least it wasn't Darius. One of the other soldiers wrenched her hands together in front of her and snapped metal shackles together over her wrists. He pushed her across the floor towards the two prisoners, and her foot caught against something and she stumbled.

She wasn't hurt, but she knew that something dreadful had happened. She felt the coldness of the water against her skin. The water had been spilled. There might not be enough left…

The soldier chained her next to the old man, not next to the Countess as she hoped.

She was hardly able to breathe for fear.

"Enough delays," said the Pyromancer. "Are you going to stay for this, my Lord?"

The Earl, paper white, nodded.

The Pyromancer raised his hands once more.

The fireflies screamed.

CHAPTER 19

The Pyromancer

Outside, in the streets of Bricus, Max watched Laura being admitted to the palace. She looked very small beside the soldiers, tiny against the immense scale of the building.

It was still raining. Yet again, he looked up into the sky. The shadows of clouds passed over his face. There was something very desolate about this rain, although at first he had been so glad of it. There was something now which disturbed him more than he could say.

Was it just that he was frantically worried about Laura? Or was it something else? And as the rain fell on his face, at last it fell into place. He knew what had happened. Wincy was doing it. Wincy was making it rain.

And this could not be done lightly. He knew enough of aquemancy to recognize a sacrifice. This was Wincy's final act. When the link to this reality was burned up by the fireflies, she had only one remaining resource. She could make it rain, but only at tremendous cost. She had put everything into it. Everything.

He knew Wincy was dead. There was water falling all over him, the sky filled with racing clouds.

There were streams of water running through the streets. The gutters were all overflowing, the drains gurgling. The river was riding high now, swollen with the brown, rushing torrent.

At the end of the street where he stood, a small group of children were splashing each other, stamping in puddles, shrieking with laughter and excitement. Other people were standing buckets and saucepans outside to collect water. No one expected the torrent to last.

One of the children had made a paper boat and it bobbed down the street, past Max's feet. The children hurtled after it, noisily pushing and shoving.

He turned back to the palace, where the soldiers still paced along the brick battlements, and thought of Laura, risking so much, like Wincy. He felt useless, waiting outside in the rain. What could he do to help? How would he even know whether she was all right or not?

There had to be something he could do. He began to walk towards the palace, his boots splashing through the wetness.

The fireflies began to circle lower and lower over the three prisoners.

Laura tore her eyes away from the monsters.

"Countess!" she whispered, and Philomena's eyes widened, very briefly, to see the unstoppered bottles in Laura's breast pocket.

She closed her eyes for a little while, a look of intense concentration on her face. A half murmur, a few words that were not at all audible. And Laura was aware of the pull, the tugging insistence of the words, more vivid and powerful than she had ever experienced in Quinland's company. It was scrabbling at the edges of her attention, almost enough to overwhelm her thoughts.

And immediately, even as the fireflies gathered themselves for a devastating blaze of flame, a thin stream of vapour arose from one of the bottles in her jacket.

It happened so fast that Laura was never quite sure what had happened.

The vapour burst into life, suddenly and wildly.

It was Quinland, coming out fighting, a vivid figure of flooding blues and greens, bringing stormy clouds of water with him, great drenching fountains and spouting jets.

Laura saw him for only an instant.

The fireflies screamed, a high-pitched scrape of sound like chalk on a blackboard, hugely amplified. They were flung back against the glass walls with terrific force by the presence of so much gushing water. The Pyromancer was shouting, enraged, and the soldiers rushed forward, swords drawn.

But Quinland was hardly visible under his drenching screen and the soldiers couldn't get anywhere near him. There seemed to be water everywhere, and one of the fireflies had fallen to the ground, its wings melting into a sticky sludge, the dazzling colours muted and subdued by the splashing water.

The others were unaffected. They were perched back on their high rafters, screaming in wild arabesques of terror. The Pyromancer raised his arms once more, calling them to order in his strange, hissing voice.

One of them, more reckless than the others, launched itself into the air, swooping towards the fountain of water protecting Quinland.

It exhaled a vast desert wind of burning flame as it came.

The two forces met and billowing clouds of steam fizzled and hissed, and for a while no one could see anything. But when the haze dissipated, Laura could see that this second firefly was now disabled, collapsed on the ground like a soggy balloon. It raised the remnants of its head from the black mess and howled at the Pyromancer. It was trying to drag itself over the soaking floor towards him.

Without hesitation the Pyromancer tipped over one of the free-standing candelabra. The torches and candles all fell directly into the ruins of the firefly and it began to seethe, to bubble and shift.

Laura knew what was going to happen. In minutes the thing would burst into life once more, and then what would Quinland do? And all those other fireflies, screaming from the rafters. He was in no state to fight. The screen of water was draining away into miserable puddles on the floor. There was a disorientated look in his eyes that frightened Laura more than the ruin of his right arm, charred black and hanging useless at one side. He gave her a sketchy smile, but his attention was focused on the Countess. Her mouth was moving, and a gentle stream of words undercut the sound of firefly screaming.

Darius saw the fireflies waiting to attack from their beam. The Pyromancer was approaching the black sludge on the floor, a torch in his hand. That'll soon put a stop to the prisoners' tricks, he thought. They'll soon learn who is master here.

He was so transfixed by the situation that he almost didn't notice the wafting bluey-green shape appearing in front of him.

"Open the door..."

At first Darius saw nothing. And then gradually the air between him and the Countess hazed over, becoming tinged with colour. "Open the door..."

Darius heard it again. A strangely compelling whisper from a half-transparent figure, emerging from the air in front of him. Darius blinked, shaking his head, trying to clear his sight.

There was a man standing there, someone who seemed somewhat indistinct round the edges, as if the colour of his clothes and skin was bleeding away into the air.

He looked oddly familiar.

Where had he come from? Who was he? Darius hesitated, his sword drawn. Another one of those treacherous aquemancers? The blue shadowy figure was drifting towards him, and as he approached, a few drops of water, not more than half a cup, splashed through the visor of Darius's helmet, straight into his eyes.

A moment of confusion, of stinging, stabbing pain as the mists in his mind cleared.

And he saw Randall standing there before him,

with all the other fireflies swooping through the air behind him. Darius flung open the door without hesitation, and Randall, looking so strangely insubstantial, vanished through it.

A funnel of fire darted after him, wasting no time on Darius. There was no need. There were other fireflies emerging from the black sludge, revived by the Pyromancer's actions.

He hardly understood what was happening. He only knew that he had been gripped in a dream, a dream with no sense or logic about it. And the dream was now over.

"Darius!" someone shouted, a voice he knew better than any other.

He saw Laura, chained, shackled to the Countess and the old man. And near them, a figure he did not understand wavered, darting across the floor to one of the reviving fireflies. There was a brief conflagration, a tangle of flesh and scales, clouded from sight by swathes of steam. A scream, a bubbling firefly wail as it sank back into the sludge. Darius couldn't work out what had happened to the shadowy figure.

There was only one firefly left in the room now. It was limping across the floor towards Laura and the Countess. Darius cursed, about to dash over, when his shoulder was seized in a deadly grip.

The Pyromancer had got him and for a second his grip on his own identity slipped as the

Pyromancer's hot, evil breath wafted over his face. He felt the old chains of obedience and training binding him.

No. Laura was there, Laura needed him. He shook the man's hand away and wrenched at the sunburst helmet he wore. Some memory, some distant dream prompted him. He knew the Pyromancer's visor concealed something important...

With a clatter the helmet fell to the floor.

A dragon's head darted at him, spitting venom straight into his eyes. But he was already falling to one side, breathless with shock. He heard Laura call out again and rolled over towards her.

He found himself being hauled to his feet by the Earl. The man's face was white with fury, his mouth clamped tight shut. He took no notice at all of what had happened to the Pyromancer. It was as if the Earl and all the other soldiers had expected this transformation.

The creature known as the Pyromancer had discarded its robes. The swathes of gold and scarlet fell in a heap on the floor and a scaled creature of claws and wings scraped across the floor towards them at great speed, and there was a moment of sheer panic as Laura and the Countess folded themselves around each other and the old man.

Darius still had his sword. He rushed at it, but other soldiers, his *friends*, held him back.

"Look at it! Look at it!" he shouted. "Can't you see what it is?"

But he saw then the flames still burning at the back of his friends' eyes, still burning in the Earl's face, and knew it was no good.

"Laura!" he cried. "I'm sorry!"

"Marrin!" It was the Countess.

The dragon was stretching its vast wings towards her, as if it might swallow her up in the embrace of scales and sharply scented breath. "Husssssh woman," its dry voice whispered like leaves sliding across stone. "Look at me..."

At that very moment the remaining firefly sprang from the rafters. The Countess and her father had to fling themselves backwards to avoid the savage blast of heat, and Laura found her feet slipping from beneath her, pulling her off balance.

Even in the chaos she found herself wondering what had happened to Quinland. The blast of flame from the firefly had scorched the floor and wall behind them. Screaming like a lunatic, it flew back up to the rafters. Laura frantically scanned the room but Quin wasn't there.

The Earl had pushed past the dragon Pyromancer and was shouting at his wife, accusing her of treachery and enchantment and evil magic.

Lord Dulchimer spoke for the first time now. He seemed almost undisturbed by the presence of the Pyromancer. His voice was old and crackly, but very clear. Laura suddenly remembered, even in this moment of extreme stress, that Max had called him powerful. Perhaps he had been the one to rescue those few drops of water after Wincy's "execution", managing to hide away the Countess's link in the fountain.

Lord Dulchimer was still talking. "Oh, no, Marrin. Don't deceive yourself. You were jealous of Philomena, aware that she was a better aquemancer than you could ever be. It's in her blood, and not in yours. It wouldn't be the first time a man's pride has been threatened."

"How dare you?" Marrin lifted his hand, indicating the dragon. "Finish it, Lerris," he said softly. "I've had enough."

The dragon's head glared at them, its eyes small, mad and furious, its breath rank and steamy. Its skin was covered in scales, overlapping halfmoons of gold and orange, and it reared up, the height of a man, ready to strike.

It resembled a firefly, but not exactly. This was a creature of flesh and blood, solidly present. This was no unstable being of gas and air. Its massive claws cut great scars into the marble floor. It was circling the prisoners, fury and hatred burning in its eyes.

And around them, members of the guard were undergoing a similar transformation. Not all of them: a few soldiers stayed at their posts, gazing impassively ahead, while their colleagues sloughed off uniforms like a second skin. They were a strange mixture, some more serpent-like than others. Only a few had dragon wings, although all had shiny scales overlapping their faces and bodies. The hall was filled with the sound of wings flapping, of claws scraping against the hard stone, of steam hissing and burning.

The Countess, at Laura's side, suddenly gripped her arm. "Look," she whispered, and Laura briefly glanced away from the approaching dragon to one of the pillars at the side.

Like a twining wisp of steam, more intricate, more delicate than before, Quinland grew into power in subtle ways, dipping and weaving.

There was something different about him. He was not quite real. Faintly transparent, fading as she looked. It was all wrong. Laura couldn't see Quinland at all clearly. He was wavering there, insubstantial as a wraith.

It was strangely fascinating. And the remaining firefly on the rafters and the others, the more fleshy ones on the ground, all of them began to converge on that one, frail figure.

"What can he do?" Laura whispered.

The odds were hopeless.

"Nothing," said the Countess.

CHAPTER 20

Deluge

Max skirted round the perimeter of the palace, looking for a way in. There seemed to be some kind of ceremony going on, for there were fewer guards on duty than usual.

The rain was pelting down. Max knew that it was almost as good as fog for disguising movement. He thought of Wincy with gratitude. But how long would the rain keep up, how long could he rely on her protection?

He knew that the tall brick wall to his left was the perimeter of the barracks. He examined the surface. The bricks were old and pitted, but there were no handholds. There was a door, quite a humble entrance a little further along, just beyond one of the buttresses. He was about to try the handle when he heard footsteps on the other side.

There was nowhere to run: the buttress blocked his way. Cursing silently, he pressed himself flat against the wall. If anyone with half their wits about them came through the door, he'd be noticed.

The door opened and a man came through.

He was no soldier. His cuffs were made of fine lace and his hair was grizzled. He was wearing glasses. He looked up and immediately sighed, taking off his pince-nez and rubbing them irritably on his handkerchief.

Max went for it. As the man fiddled with his glasses, he slipped behind him into the palace.

This was clearly a back door. There was a flight of stairs right in front of him and Max sprinted up them, to get well out of the way before the short-sighted man returned.

He reached the top of the stairs and ran along the corridor. Then he heard footsteps coming towards him and men's voices talking loudly, sharing a joke.

He dived, without hesitation, into the room on his right.

"Who are you? What are you doing here?" There was a pale-faced youth sitting up in bed there, staring at him.

Max didn't speak. He pressed his finger to his lips and stood behind the door, very quietly. The youth stared at him, his mouth slightly open. He said nothing.

Max exhaled. "Thank you," he murmured. "I owe you one."

"Tell me what you're doing," the youth said. "Explain."

"I'm looking for a friend of mine. She came to see the Pyromancer – "

"*She?* Suicidal, is she? Women aren't popular round here."

"It was a risk, I know. But Laura said—"

"Laura? Darius Brooke's sister?"

Max stared at him. "You know Darius?"

The youth nodded. "My name's Franklin," he said. "Who are you? Had you better tell me all about it?"

Franklin wasn't too steady on his feet, but he knew his way round the palace. He led Max first to the uniform store where they both dressed as soldiers, and then away from the barracks and across the quad into the main part of the palace. While Max waited in the shadows, Franklin asked one of the soldiers on guard there why it was so quiet. What was going on?

Franklin returned to Max, his face pale. "Executions," he said blankly. "The Countess and her father are due to be executed any moment now. In the Pyromancer's quarters."

Max was thinking fast. "Not out in the square as usual?"

"No, it's raining too hard. The fireflies can't tolerate water."

"Where are the Pyromancer's quarters?"

"To the north of the palace. The glasshouse, we call it."

"The glasshouse – ?"

"The Pyromancer likes the heat. He won't be enjoying this wet spell…"

Thoughtfully, they looked through the window at the rain still sheeting down.

"This way," said Franklin suddenly. "I've got an idea."

The palace was completely surrounded by the high brick wall. The glass towers and roofs were protected by this barrier of brick, with its battlements and cannon emplacements.

They met no one on the way up to the battlements, but there were guards on duty at the top, bored-looking men overlooking the drenched city. Franklin and Max marched swiftly along the battlements, trying not to look nervous. No one gave them a second glance.

As they got nearer to the glass roofs over the Pyromancer's quarters, the rain intensified. They could see great pools of water gathering in the angles between the slope of the many roofs.

They could see, in one section, that steam was clouding the glass, as if a furnace were burning there.

"That's it," said Max. "That's got to be it. All that steam … fireflies and aquemancers, don't you think?"

"We haven't much time," Franklin said and Max nodded, white-faced. He knew it was a risk, a terrible chance they were taking.

"Come on then," said Franklin and together they raced round the battlements until they came to one of the heavy iron cannons, unguarded, unprotected.

There was no one nearby. They bent down over it and knocked away the blocks keeping it in place. The cannon began to roll the wrong way, towards the outer wall. Trying to keep quiet, they braced their feet against the brick and leaned their shoulders against the gun and it steadied, standing still for just a second before beginning to roll the other way.

Max and Franklin stood together on the edge of the battlements and watched as the cannon dropped through the air, spinning over once, twice, until it crashed right through the steamy roof of the main chamber.

It shattered through the roof and a great river of

water from the gulleys in the roof went with it.

The noise was immense, the rush of steam and flame rising far above the battlements. People were shouting, running, Max and Franklin with them.

There was no way to tell who had survived.

The roof shattered. Something exploded against the glass and it fell apart in a thousand jagged shards. No one from below had any opportunity to realize what it was. The ceiling was imploding, shattering in showers of flickering light towards them. The object landed in the midst of the fireflies with an enormous crash, and water cascaded over them all.

It caught the huge beast which had been the Pyromancer in the centre of its body. The creature squealed and wriggled, unable to escape, and they all saw that the falling object was a cannon, its barrel pointing up to the sky.

The Pyromancer could not escape. Blood, more orange than crimson, pumped across the floor in steaming gushes. As the rainwater bit into its scales, the dragon began to writhe, to whip back on itself in curving figure-of-eight shapes until the frantic movement stilled.

The other serpents, ex-members of the Guard and pyromancy, shrivelled up as if drenched in acid as the rainwater washed over them.

Laura and the Countess and Lord Dulchimer clutched each other as they watched the devastation. There was glass all over and around them, but miraculously none of them was hurt.

On the far side of the hall, the Earl was safely out of the way. The remaining soldiers round the walls were untouched, too.

Only the Pyromancer and its serpent followers had perished in the deluge.

Silence. The Countess said, at last, "Marrin? Are you all right?"

Her husband was distracted, bewildered. He looked as if he could believe nothing. "Philomena? My God, what – I was about to have you *executed*!"

He crossed the hall towards them, stepping clear of the black sludge and the still twitching remains of the dragon. His face was white with shock, his hands shaking as he fumbled with keys and unlocked the chains.

As soon as she was released, Laura ran over to Darius and helped him take off his helmet.

Like Marrin, he seemed in a state of shock. He wrapped his arms round her like a drowning man. "Laura, this has been impossible, all madness…"

Together, at the same moment, they remembered someone else. They looked round at the devastation.

"But how … how did that get here?" Darius indicated the cannon, tipped on one side, its great barrel still pointing up to the gaping hole in the ceiling. No one looked at the remains of the Pyromancer, crushed there.

"And what about Quinland?"

"I think that Quinland has left us," said the Countess, from the other side of the room. "That final manifestation took all his remaining energy. Like Wincy, he gave everything." She sounded serious, although her fingers reached for Marrin's hand as she spoke. They moved closer together, and still the rain drummed down around them.

chapter 21

Death Dreams

The dragon was dead, the Earl and his Guard restored to themselves.

Laura surveyed the devastation and found, standing by the door, someone she recognized.

Max, his hair plastered down by the rain, out of breath and laughing. "My God!" he shouted. "Bullseye!"

"It was you!" Laura hugged him. "You made that cannon fall!"

"I had help," he said lightly. "Is this all of them?" He indicated the remains of the fireflies, and Laura suddenly remembered.

"Randall!" said Laura urgently. "We have to help him…"

They ran together to the double doors and out into the corridor.

Randall had one aim in mind. To get the fireflies out of the palace and into the wet. He could still hear rainfall drumming down on the ceilings and against the windows. He didn't know what had happened to Wincy but he could guess. He didn't mourn.

He knew he was dying, too. He knew that vital essences had been lost, irreplaceably lost. He had so little energy, so little strength. It took everything he had to open a window, to push against a door. He could feel cold draughts of air passing through him, a deep chill that struck deeper than the inertia of being caught in the dreaming. When he looked at his own hand, he saw that it was transparent, like a veil of flesh.

But the plan had worked, for the Earl was disenchanted, the Pyromancer destroyed. It was going to be all right – so long as he could get the last fireflies into the rain.

He didn't know the palace. He had some sense of direction, but it was not much use. There were soldiers at every door, standing guard at every junction. He found himself running up and down staircases, tending somehow or other towards the outer perimeter.

He knew that he was lucky, that the fireflies

would certainly have caught him if he had materialized a little earlier. Quinland had done that. Quinland had given him this chance, just as Wincy, lost for ever in a dream of rainwater, was going to be responsible for the death of the fireflies.

He could hear them roaring after him, and knew that they could catch him in an instant if they wanted to. But there was something feline about fireflies, something playful. They were allowing him to run, knowing that in the end there was no possible escape.

And although he had a head start, Randall was well aware that this was worth next to nothing. The breath coming from the fireflies was as lethal, as potent as ever.

And he was dying. At every step his energy drained away. He knew he was leaving behind him footprints dark with water. In water, his life was draining away.

Max, Darius and Laura were not far behind. They pounded down the long corridors, and up wide-curving staircases, never pausing. Neither Max nor Laura were familiar with the lay-out of the palace, but Darius seemed to know what was ahead.

"He's making for the quad," he gasped.

Laura didn't understand the significance, didn't

know why Darius was looking so hopeful.

She skidded suddenly, her feet swerving, slipping away from her. Laura found herself reaching out for Max's shoulder to prevent herself from losing balance.

They kept running. But something made her glance back and for a moment the mad pace of the chase halted.

She saw a shadow form, something at once familiar and strange. A shape like Randall, fading into the blue shadows at the side of the corridor. It *was* Randall, she knew it, no one else looked like that, blond hair in such disarray, tall and lean beneath the ragged clothes...

And it could not be Randall. The real Randall was still running, far ahead of them, leading the fireflies away... A running figure without substance, leaving behind imprints, vague shadows of his real self. The pattern of stones in the wall shone through the transparent likeness. Randall the dream, she thought crazily. Randall the fading reflection.

She didn't understand. But she knew it was dangerous, that this was no natural trans-formation. And the exhilaration that had gripped her, the joy at finding Darius once more, became submerged in anxiety.

They fled down the stone corridors towards yet another staircase. At its bottom another figure, another fading representation of their cousin, clung to the wall, draining away in pale cascades.

Water splashed on the floor at her feet. A breath on the air, something half heard, half sensed.

Farewell.

Randall was gone. She knew it. He had lost too much substance in the transformation and could no longer hold it together. Her cousin was dead.

"Laura! Come on!" Max was hauling on her hand, pulling her away.

There was no longer any need to pursue the fireflies. In fact, the sensible thing would be to get as far from them as possible. They saw the fireflies racing ahead of them, whizzing down the tight curves to a spiral staircase. They left great swathes of sparks behind them, a carpet of fire to catch and snare at their feet. With a shriek, the fireflies blazed through the door which stood open at the bottom of the staircase.

They dashed out along the colonnade. There was someone there already, a soldier Laura didn't recognize. At her side Darius suddenly shouted, "Perrian! For God's sake, Perrian, look out!"

But Darius's friend, with his severe face and short haircut, only smiled. He reached out his hands towards the fireflies and Laura saw, aghast, that his skin was scaled, covered in repeating half-moon shapes of gold and scarlet.

From above, it looked as if there was something

reptilian in the wry action of his neck, something in those flat eyes and heavy bones that reminded her –

Laura remembered how fireflies grew from the death of humans, remembered that the Pyromancer had seemed human too. We're very close to them, she thought. The edges are blurred, perhaps this is what will happen to us all one day...

She clung to Max. She said, "Oh, Max, what are they, what are they?"

And it was Darius who answered her.

"A hybrid," he said. "A mess. Something not one thing nor another. A distortion."

"*Liar!*" Perrian hissed, quite at ease next to the fireflies. Now they had paused, Laura could see for the first time that there were three of them.

Darius took a step downwards. One of the fireflies flared at him, but Perrian put out his hand, or whatever it was, to hold it back.

There were strange elongated nails to his fingers, strange hanging folds of material or skin between arm and side. *Claws*, said Laura's mind. Claws, and wings.

"Perrian," said Darius, and there was something sad in his voice, something Laura had never heard before. "Perrian, the Pyromancer is dead."

She had never heard him sound so serious before. She looked at her brother as if she had never known him.

There was a snarl, a rictus on Perrian's face, something savage and shocking. His clawed hand moved to a pouch hanging from his belt and with an action too quick to understand, he flung a handful of spicy powder straight in their faces.

It was Darius, standing further down the staircase, who received the brunt of it. He bent double, sneezing and coughing, his eyes streaming.

"My father!" snarled the creature Darius had called Perrian. "My father, dead?"

The Pyromancer. The Pyromancer was Perrian's father.

"The Pyromancer cannot die!" he screamed. "You are deceived!"

"No." Max this time. He was speaking coldly, clearly. "The ceiling fell in. There was water everywhere. The Pyromancer is finished, like a worm on a griddle. And you now are caught between the weeping sky and us. You cannot survive here."

"How stupid you are, how stupid are all men! What can you do against usssss?"

With horror, Laura saw that Max was preparing to launch himself at Perrian, armed only with his knife.

She grabbed his arm. "No! You can't!"

For the fireflies were fizzing dangerously, infuriated by the delay.

"Over here!" A new voice, someone she didn't

251

recognize. Through the stone colonnades at the bottom of the staircase she could see someone standing in the rain, bareheaded. He seemed unsteady, possibly unwell, and there were the marks on his face of burns.

For a moment it looked as if Perrian was distracted.

He snarled at Darius, "Oh, look, it's your low-life friend poking his nose in where he's not wanted." He raised his voice. "Come out of the rain, Franklin! Come and join the fun!"

Darius straightened up. From behind, Laura couldn't see his face. He walked slowly and steadily down the stairs to join Perrian, showing no fear at all of the fireflies sparking dangerously beneath the stone arches.

She thought, oh, no, it's that powder, it's got hold of Darry again. At her side, she could feel Max hesitate.

"Go back, Laura," he said. "Go and get help."

"No, I can't let Darius go again."

She whisked away from him and ran downstairs. At the back of her mind she thought the man in the quad will help, he'll do something to distract them...

But through the stone arches she could see him running away and her heart sank as the creature called Perrian came forward to grasp her with his horrible, clawed hands.

"Who is this, Darius?" Perrian hissed. "Do you know this woman?"

She saw her brother stare at her with blank eyes, unrecognizing, unfamiliar.

"No. Should I?"

"Darius!" she shouted. "Don't do this, you're drugged, you *know* me!"

But his eyes passed indifferently over her, towards the rain-sodden quad.

She could feel the breath of the fireflies swirling round them in eddies of sulphurous heat. They were twitching, maddened by the enforced stillness. And Perrian's control seemed limited at best. She knew they were about to attack, that this was merely a brief respite.

It was only a matter of time. Glancing back up the staircase, Laura saw that Max had vanished too. Gone for help, she thought dismally. But he'll be too late, it's too late…

She turned back to Darius, and was appalled by the change in him, the dead look to his face.

And when he acted, it was so sudden that she was caught off balance. Between one moment of stillness and the next he had seized her round the waist, throwing them both over the edge of the colonnade out into the soaking quad.

They fell in a rolling heap into the mud, and then that other man was there, the man called Franklin. He had his hands full of buckets and there was water sloshing everywhere.

Without thinking, acting so fast that she had no time for fear, Laura took one of the buckets and hurled it at the gap between the colonnades.

It was accurate. The water splashed all over the fireflies and they collapsed like pricked balloons. Perrian was shielding his own face and the water seemed to have no effect on him. He gave a yell and threw himself out into the quad, his sword drawn, running straight at Darius.

Perrian always won. At the back of his mind, Darius remembered that he had never defeated Perrian in their training sessions. He'd never come anywhere near it. Perrian was stronger, more lithe, more agile. And now that the true shape of his hands was revealed, now that the claws were no longer sheathed by his human disguise, Darius could not afford to get too close.

They circled each other warily. "How did you do it? How could you fool us all?" said Darius. He wanted to know, but he also wanted to distract Perrian. He would have to rely on more than physical strength to defeat Perrian.

"It was easy," Perrian said and in the dim, rain-filled light, Darius saw the metallic sheen of his skin. How had he missed it before, this reptilian quality?

Perrian supplied the answer. "It's in the sessera.

The red powder on the food, the powder makes the smoke. We get it from the ashes of dead humans, after we have fed..." He laughed at the look on Darius's face. "Think," he said slowly. "We – the fireflies – reproduce when humans die. And when enough humans have died, when we have fed over and over again, then we too become partly human. And the ashes, the left-over remains, have this power to deceive you and your fellows... You can be controlled with the spice..."

As he spoke, his clawed hand crept towards the pouch on his belt. Darius was waiting for this: he flung himself to one side as the red powder stained the air over his head.

Perrian attacked, and from his position on the ground, Darius had to block him with his upraised sword. He felt the force of Perrian's blow judder all along his arm. He rolled over in the mud and surged to his feet, just in time to avoid a slicing sword aimed at his neck. He ran at Perrian then, and the swords clashed in a shower of sparks. He saw Perrian grinning at him, and felt the hot, spicy breath in his nose and mouth.

They broke loose and started to circle once more.

Another clash, and this time Perrian forced him to give way, staggering back into the mud. He knew that Perrian was effortlessly superior at this.

And then his foot slipped. He felt himself falling and knew that Perrian was running, raising his sword –

He saw Perrian fall towards him, a look of vast surprise on his scaled face, the eyes wide and blank.

Perrian fell on top of him, and with terrified shock, Darius saw the arrow jutting from his back.

With disgust, he pushed the body off and scrambled to his feet. Over the other side of the quad Franklin was lowering his bow.

And then Laura was running towards him, her arms held wide, and he knew it was over, that the dream was finished and the power of the Pyromancer destroyed. He held her close, shuddering with reaction.

CHAPTER 22

Dream Worlds

At the banquet, Laura and Darius sat together. Max was on Laura's right hand, Nina next to Darius. Franklin was placed beside Nina, and was too shy to say much. Laura saw Nina cast sideways glances at Darius and realized with some amusement that her brother had recovered some of his old confidence. He was beginning to show off.

They all raised their glasses as the Earl stood up and pledged a toast to the Countess Philomena under the approving eye of Lord Dulchimer.

And Philomena raised her glass too and widened the gesture to include Laura and Max, to Darius and Nina and Franklin.

Around them sat men clothed in scarlet and gold. Their visors were gone. Their eyes gazed steadily at the crowds and the feast laid out on the tables and it seemed impossible to remember the flames that had gleamed behind the visors.

Marrin had discovered the stockpile of sessera that the Pyromancer had stored away in its quarters. Without regret he had destroyed it all, taking the advice of his wife and her councillors, the aquemancers. It had been encased in iron and dropped to the bottom of the deepest lake in all of Bricus.

Sometimes in the night it rained. Laura would stir in her sleep, although she did not awake as the night air cooled.

In her dream she was in the country once more. It was night-time. She stood there in a grassy meadow waiting, and brief rags of cloud scudded across the face of the moon. In its wavering light she saw three figures far across the calm field.

Fading, one moment there, the next uncertain. A gleam of shining hair, a warm-eyed smile, the wave of a hand... Wincy, Quinland and Randall, talking to each other, engaged in a vivid and important conversation. They were drifting through the night air in disappearing clouds of soft rain, in a dreaming world Laura did not yet understand.

One day she would. Philomena had promised to give her instruction in aquemancy, so that she might inherit the legacy of Alderwood blood. One day she might understand the dreaming, and then perhaps she might be able to talk with them once again...

She sighed and turned over, and slept until morning.

Encounter worlds where men and women make hazardous voyages through space; where time travel is a reality and the fifth dimension a possibility; where the ultimate horror has already happened and mankind breaks through the barrier of technology...

Read Point SF and enter a new dimension...

Point Horror

Are you hooked on horror? Are you thrilled by fear? Then these are the books for you! A powerful series of horror fiction designed to keep you quaking in your shoes.

Titles available now:

The Cemetery
D.E. Athkins

The Dead Game
Mother's Helper
A. Bates

The Cheerleader
The Return of the Vampire
The Vampire's Promise
Freeze Tag
The Perfume
The Stranger
Twins
Caroline B. Cooney

April Fools
The Lifeguard
The Mall
Teacher's Pet
Trick or Treat
Richie Tankersley Cusick

Camp Fear
My Secret Admirer
Silent Witness
The Window
Carol Ellis

The Accident
The Invitation
The Fever
Funhouse
The Train
Nightmare Hall:
The Silent Scream
Deadly Attraction
The Roommate
The Wish
Guilty
The Scream Team
Diane Hoh

The Yearbook
Peter Lerangis

The Watcher
Lael Littke

The Forbidden Game:
The Hunter
The Chase
L.J. Smith

Dream Date
The Diary
The Waitress
Sinclair Smith

The Phantom
Barbara Steiner

The Baby-sitter
The Baby-sitter II
The Baby-sitter III
Beach House
Beach Party
The Boyfriend
Call Waiting
The Dead Girlfriend
The Girlfriend
Halloween Night
The Hitchhiker
Hit and Run
The Snowman
The Witness
R.L. Stine

Thirteen Tales of Horror
Various
Thirteen More Tales of Horror
Various
Thirteen Again
Various

Look out for:

Fatal Secrets
Richie Tankersley Cusick

Driver's Dead
Peter Lerangis

The Boy Next Door
Sinclair Smith

A terrifying series from Point Horror!

NIGHTMARE HALL

Where college is a

scream ...

High on a hill overlooking Salem
University, hidden in shadows and
shrouded in mystery, sits Nightingale Hall.

Nightmare Hall, the students call it.

Because that's where the terror began ...

Don't miss the spine-tingling thrillers in
the Nightmare Hall series –

The Silent Scream
The Roommate
Deadly Attraction
The Wish
Guilty

P●INT CRiME

If you like Point Horror, you'll love Point Crime!

A murder has been committed . . . Whodunnit?
Was it the teacher, the schoolgirl, or the best friend? An
exciting series of crime novels, with tortuous plots and lots
of suspects, designed to keep the reader guessing till the
very last page.

Kiss of Death
School for Death
Peter Beere

Avenging Angel
Break Point
Final Cut
Shoot the Teacher
The Beat:
Missing Person
Black and Blue
Devid Belbin

Baa Baa Dead Sheep
Jill Bennett

A Dramatic Death
Margaret Bingley

Driven to Death
Patsy Kelly Investigates:
A Family Affair
Anne Cassidy

Overkill
Alane Ferguson

Deadly Music
Death Penalty
Dennis Hamley

Concrete Evidence
The Smoking Gun
Malcolm Rose

Dance With Death
Jean Ure

Point

Pointing the way forward

More compelling reading from top authors.

Flight 116 is Down
Forbidden
Unforgettable
Caroline B. Cooney

Someone Else's Baby
Geraldine Kaye

Hostilities
Caroline Macdonald

I Carried You On Eagles' Wings
Sue Mayfield

Seventeenth Summer
K.M. Peyton

The Highest Form of Killing
Son of Pete Flude
Malcolm Rose

Secret Lives
William Taylor